RECEIVED

MADRONA

BIRDIE'S BILLIONS

BIRDIE'S BILLIONS

EDITH COHN

BLOOMSBURY
CHILDREN'S BOOKS
NEW YORK LONDON OXFORD NEW DELHI SYDNEY

BLOOMSBURY CHILDREN'S BOOKS
Bloomsbury Publishing Inc., part of Bloomsbury Publishing Plc
1385 Broadway, New York, NY 10018

BLOOMSBURY, BLOOMSBURY CHILDREN'S BOOKS, and the Diana logo are trademarks of
Bloomsbury Publishing Plc

First published in the United States of America in November 2021
by Bloomsbury Children's Books
www.bloomsbury.com

Bloomsbury books may be purchased for business or promotional use.
For information on bulk purchases please contact Macmillan Corporate and
Premium Sales Department at specialmarkets@macmillan.com

Library of Congress Cataloging-in-Publication Data
Names: Cohn, Edith, author.
Title: Birdie's billions / by Edith Cohn.
Description: New York: Bloomsbury Children's Books, 2021.
Summary: When Birdie discovers cash in an abandoned house, she thinks it could be the
answer to her and her mother's problems, but she wonders about the people who left that
money behind and tries to figure what is best for her family and what is the right thing to do.
Identifiers: LCCN 2021018104 (print) | LCCN 2021018105 (e-book)
ISBN 978-1-5476-0711-2 (hardcover) | ISBN 978-1-5476-0782-2 (e-book)
Subjects: CYAC: Lost and found possessions—Fiction. | Behavior—Fiction. | Mystery and
detective stories. | LCGFT: Detective and mystery fiction.
Classification: LCC PZ7.C66493 Bi 2021 (print) | LCC PZ7.C66493 (e-book) | DDC [Fic]—dc23
LC record available at https://lccn.loc.gov/2021018104
LC e-book record available at https://lccn.loc.gov/2021018105

Book design by Jeanette Levy
Typeset by Westchester Publishing Services
Printed and bound in the U.S.A.
2 4 6 8 10 9 7 5 3 1

To find out more about our authors and books visit
www.bloomsbury.com and sign up for our newsletters.

For Tatra

BIRDIE'S BILLIONS

1

Birdie tried to concentrate on her math homework as the familiar smell of orange dust spray and lemon floor polish made a chemical fruit basket in her nose.

Mama waved a cloth in Birdie's direction. "Can you help me with this curio cabinet?"

Birdie jumped up. She would take any excuse not to do math word problems, even if it meant dusting. "How do you know this thing is called a curio cabinet?" Mrs. Hillmore's house was filled with fancy oddities like the huge glass case in front of her, which had a light shining down on dozens of breakable figurines.

"I don't know. I guess the same way I know curio is

short for curiosity." Mama handed Birdie a porcelain figure of two kids holding a sand pail. "Maybe I learned it watching *Downton Abbey*."

Downton Abbey was Mama's favorite TV show featuring a family of British nobles. "Right! The Crawleys probably have tons of curio cabinets."

Mama gave Birdie a sly smile like they were in on a secret together. "You know they do, along with thirty maids to dust them."

"Poor Mrs. Hillmore with just us to take care of everything."

Mama laughed. "She'll have to survive."

Birdie took all the figurines out of the case, cleaned the glass bottoms of the cabinet, and put them back inside, being extra careful with a wobbly ice skater precariously perched on one leg. Then she sat back down at Mrs. Hillmore's enormous table, which had too many chairs, to finish her homework.

But she couldn't stop fidgeting.

She followed Mama to the basement where she was taking out Mrs. Hillmore's laundry from the dryer. "Can I borrow your phone or Mrs. Hillmore's to see if Hailey's home?" Mrs. Hillmore still had a house phone, so if she could use that, she wouldn't waste any of Mama's minutes. "I want to skateboard over there." Her best friend Hailey lived near Mrs. Hillmore's house, and it was always so fun to zip super-fast on the wide, smooth streets in the nicest neighborhood in Valley Lake.

Mama stopped pulling out the laundry and turned toward Birdie. "I want you to stay inside today. I'll drive you to Hailey's tomorrow."

"What? Why?" Birdie had brought her board, and the weather was nice. Sure, Mama had to work on Saturdays, but Birdie didn't. She could finish her homework tomorrow.

"I'm sorry," Mama said. "It's safer to stay inside."

It didn't make any sense. The whole reason they'd moved to Valley Lake was because it was so safe. They had great public schools, and Mama could make twice as much money cleaning for rich people. It was why Birdie had to leave all her friends and everything she knew behind. And now she was trapped inside because Mama suddenly thought it was unsafe?

The unfairness of it all bumped up inside her like the rocky, narrow streets of her own neighborhood that knocked her skateboard loose under her feet.

Back at Mrs. Hillmore's too-big table, she tried to focus on her math homework. She studied a problem about marbles—red, yellow, and blue ones, and *how many yellow ones did the kid playing with them have left after shooting half of the red ones in the bushes?* But she couldn't sit still or stop thinking about all the fun her friends were having while she was stuck at Mrs. Hillmore's. A small tornado of fury funneled up inside her.

Her skateboard was attached to the back of her bookbag with straps that Mama had sewn on special for her. The Velcro made a loud ripping sound as she pulled her skateboard loose. Mrs. Hillmore's cat heard the noise and came over to check things out. Birdie rubbed behind his soft, white ears, but he lifted his head as if to ask *is that all?*

"I'm sorry. It's just a skateboard." But to her it was everything. It could take her anywhere she wanted to go—if only she could go outside. Why wasn't she allowed?

Her fingers gripped tightly over her board and her feet itched to move. Fine. If Mama wanted to be crazy not letting her outside, she could be crazy, too. She stepped on her board and wiggled herself around a bit while the wheels stayed still. She threw out her arms, bent her knees, and imagined she was sailing over a huge set of stairs. Flying, flying, flying. Long enough to gain serious air. Long enough that she'd defied gravity. Long enough that crowds of kids had gathered around with their phones out recording her, cheering. She bowed, imagining she'd landed the trick. "Thank you! Thank you, all!"

The cat, her only actual audience, stared at her a moment, then sauntered off. He jumped to the top of the couch and turned his back to her as if she'd betrayed him.

"Okay, okay. I'll check the cabinets for some treats for you. I'm not supposed to go snooping around, but for you, I'll break the rules."

She stepped forward, wobbled, leaned the wrong way, and before she knew it, the board was out from under her feet flying toward the curio cabinet. Her body hurled backward into a side table. Everything crashed with a heavy thud.

"Birdie?" Mama shouted from downstairs.

Birdie was still on the floor when Mama reached the dining room, her eyes wide with shock. The shirt Mama had held floated to the floor as if in slow motion. "Are you okay?" Mama whispered like her voice had floated away, too.

Birdie nodded and carefully stretched out the arm she'd used to break her fall. She could move it. It wasn't broken. She stood up. She was a baby bird who'd fallen out of a tree, who with a few shakes of her feathers was stunned, but as good as new.

Together, she and Mama lifted the table that had fallen over back upright. But there was a hole where the corner had hit the wall. And it wasn't the sort of hole you wouldn't notice if you didn't know it was there. Not even if you cleaned up all the plaster pieces that had broken off onto the floor. Birdie put her hand over it. It was bigger than her palm.

"It's hollow," she marveled. She'd never seen the inside of a wall, and its hollowness was something of a shock. She could fit her whole hand inside the hole. "Did you know walls weren't solid?"

"No, I didn't," Mama said. "And I wish I didn't know now."

"Maybe we can fix it?" Though Birdie had no idea how. She looked at the side table. "Or move something in front of it?"

Mama shook her head. "We can't hide it. I'll have to tell her." Mama turned to see the skateboard wedged underneath the curio cabinet. "Were you riding your skateboard in the house?"

"No. I was just standing on it—standing still."

"Not that still," Mama said, observing the mess.

"At least nothing broke in the curio cabinet." It seemed incredibly lucky.

"I agree that's something to be grateful for. At least a wall isn't sentimental. Maybe she'll be understanding." Mama's voice lifted at the end, like she was asking a question.

Birdie had never met Mrs. Hillmore, because on days Mama cleaned, Mrs. Hillmore visited another old lady friend in a nursing home.

Birdie went to retrieve her skateboard, but it was jammed in tight at a weird angle under the cabinet. She yanked on it.

"Wait!" Mama shouted.

But it was too late. The board sprang loose with such force that Birdie fell back on her rear, and the ice skater smacked face-first into the glass, smashing into a thousand pieces.

6

Mama didn't say anything for a few seconds. A long few seconds where Birdie considered the terrible trouble her mother was going to be in now.

Finally, Mama shook her head. "What were you thinking?"

"Let me talk to Mrs. Hillmore," Birdie begged. "I'll explain it was all my fault, and she can have all the money I make at summer jobs for as long as it takes until it's paid off." Birdie didn't have a summer job, and she wasn't sure how old you had to be to have one. Still, even if it took years, she would make this right.

"No," Mama said. "You're my responsibility and so is this house while I'm here."

Mama fished her phone from the pocket of her jacket, which hung by the door. "Let's just hope Mrs. Hillmore has a forgiving spirit."

She didn't.

Birdie listened to the *yes, ma'am*s, Mama repeated while on the phone with Mrs. Hillmore with the out of control feeling of her board on a runaway hill headed into traffic. As soon as she hung up, Mama walked over to the curio cabinet and pointed to the pile of glass that used to be shaped like an ice skater. "Do you want to know how much that thing was worth?"

Birdie chewed her lip.

"Her son helped her win it on eBay for $1,300."

"Are you kidding?"

"I wish. Get your things. We're leaving."

The car ride home was miserably silent. Birdie wondered if maybe she could make cookies or her and Mama's favorite candy, buckeyes, to smooth things over. But then she thought about how the ice skater came from eBay instead of from a friend, and how Mrs. Hillmore had told Mama the price instead of how much it meant to her. It didn't seem sentimental. It only seemed expensive, which probably meant no amount of sugar was going to sweeten up mean Mrs. Hillmore. So, for once, Birdie resisted her impulses and held her tongue.

She didn't breathe a word that night, not through the remaining three math problems she had to complete for homework and not a word all through dinner. Not even when Mama's phone rang, and Birdie could tell from the way Mama jumped up to answer it that it was her boss from Clean as a Whistle. Birdie stayed perfectly silent as Mama said another series of grim *yes, ma'am*s and one *I understand*, and hung up the phone without even saying goodbye.

This wasn't good.

It sounded an awful lot like Mama had just been fired.

2

After Birdie went to bed that night, she heard the desperate whispers of Mama on her phone. She couldn't catch what Mama was saying, but the urgent sound of her voice made Birdie hug her pillow tight to her chest. Memories of the last time her mother didn't have a job resurfaced in her mind. She was only five, and her dad had gotten arrested. He didn't come back home and didn't come back home, and didn't come back home. And Mama had to figure out a way to support them. Birdie hardly remembered her dad, but what she would never forget was the look of panic in Mama's eyes when she went to pay for groceries and didn't have enough.

The next day was Sunday, and Mama had said she'd drop Birdie off at Hailey's house. But Birdie wasn't sure if that promise still stood, seeing as how she'd screwed things up so bad yesterday. Maybe she should be grounded for a few weeks . . . or a few years.

As luck would have it, at ten to two, Mama put on one of her dresses with too many flowers and grabbed her purse. "Come on. You don't deserve it after that stunt you pulled yesterday. But I have some errands to run. I'd rather not take you, and I don't want you home alone. Leave your skateboard here." Mama eyed Birdie's board like she was afraid Birdie would break a glass ice skater at Hailey's house, too.

Birdie hadn't been planning to bring her skateboard since Mama was driving her. Hailey didn't skateboard, and neither did any of the other girls at her school. It was another of the many differences between Polkville, where she'd spent most of her life, and Valley Lake. Polkville was only a two-and-a-half-hour drive away, but sometimes the two places seemed like different worlds.

"Do Hailey and I have to stay inside?" Birdie asked.

"No."

"Really?" Birdie had thought for sure Mama would say yes.

"I didn't plan for you to be cooped up forever. I'm sure it's fine to be outside by now."

Birdie didn't get why it would ever not be safe to be outside in Evercrest. It was the fanciest neighborhood in Valley Lake. They had a neighborhood watch, and the police came quickly when someone called. She wanted to ask Mama about it but decided not to press her luck. "I'm sorry I didn't listen to you before. Well, I listened. I didn't go outside, but I got mad about it."

"I'm sorry, too," Mama said, though what Mama was sorry about Birdie wasn't sure—maybe that Birdie owned a skateboard.

Usually Hailey and Birdie played in the treehouse in her backyard, but they weren't allowed to anymore. Apparently, safety was a big concern with Hailey's mom, too. So, the girls needed to find a new place to call their own.

"Maybe we should look across the lake?" Hailey asked.

There was a new housing development being built on the other side of the lake with wooden almost-houses that might be good for hanging out inside. "How are we going to get over there?" Birdie asked.

"We can borrow a canoe." Hailey motioned to the row of canoes lined up along the lake. "We'll bring it right back. No one will care."

Birdie eyed the canoes that didn't belong to them. "Really?" In butter-soft caramel fuzzy boots, Hailey didn't look dressed for canoeing.

But Hailey had a determined *don't worry about it* look across her rosy face.

"Sure. Of course. Why not?" Birdie pushed the answers to that question to the back of her mind and hurried to be the first one in the boat.

They paddled across no problem and jumped out on the other side, excited to explore all the unfinished, soon-to-be lake houses.

"This is the biggest." Birdie counted the wooden frames. It would have nine bedrooms, likely a pool, and had plenty of room for a treehouse in the yard.

"Let's buy it and furnish it with the finest." Hailey waltzed around the house on her toes with her hand out.

"We must have the biggest," Birdie agreed, playing along.

The other almost-houses, also at the moment only wood and nails, would be smaller. The poor souls who had to suffer with only eight bedrooms.

Birdie's feet pounded the wooden planks that stood in for a floor. She liked the solid sound her sneakers made as they smacked the unpolished surface.

Hailey marched around behind her in her fuzzy boots with bottoms as soft as bedroom slippers. "I can't get my shoes to make any noise."

Birdie's sneakers looked as old as her eleven years. So old, her normally neat-freak mother had forbidden them to go in the wash for fear they wouldn't live to see the dryer. Mama had said she'd take her shopping for new ones as soon as she got paid, but that most likely wouldn't be happening now. "Old, but solid." Birdie gave the wood another satisfying smack.

Hailey laughed and plopped down on the top step near where a front door might someday be hammered in and shut tight. Her friend pulled two sodas from her leather bookbag and handed one to Birdie. The girls clinked cans. "To our new house."

"To our new house."

Hailey flipped her hair from her face and took a long sip of her soda, a real one with bad chemicals and sugar.

"I love your sweater." Hailey reached over to touch the material. "The color is so unique."

"Thanks. You can borrow it if you want. It won't mind. It's used to being passed around." The sweater was an inky green. Birdie had found it at a thrift store for four dollars, which was exactly how many times she'd had to wash it before it smelled as nice as Hailey was claiming it looked.

"Thanks. I love retro," Hailey said, making Birdie's old clothes seem like a fashion choice she'd made on purpose, which made Birdie feel a lot cooler than she was.

"Someone's coming." Hailey scrambled to her feet and hid her soda behind her like the fact she was drinking it might somehow get back to her mother.

Across the lake another canoe made its way toward them. Any minute it looked like they'd have company. Two boys, one of whom, from the looks of it, was several years older than Hailey and Birdie. Hailey put her bag on her shoulder, ready to split. "Should we hide?"

Behind the unfinished houses was a forest. They could easily hide there.

Birdie stomped a determined foot on the platformed floor. "This is our house. I'm not leaving it."

Never mind that their new house didn't have walls and wasn't much good for privacy or defense. Never mind that in a few months or even weeks from now when it did have walls and a door that locked, they wouldn't be allowed inside.

Today it was theirs.

Hailey scanned the horizon and her shoulders relaxed a notch. "It's only Jacob Powers."

Jacob was in their sixth-grade class. He was a skateboarder, so Birdie had noticed him. Maybe more than noticed him. But they hadn't talked much. "Who's the other boy?"

Hailey wrinkled her nose and shrugged. Hailey had lived in Valley Lake all her life and knew everyone at Valley Lake Elementary, but this boy looked like he went to junior high.

The boys pushed their canoe into the dirt and approached. "That's Jacob's brother," Hailey said. The two boys had the same dark hair, the same confidently squared shoulders, the same easy walk. They had their skateboards at their sides, and Birdie felt a longing for her own.

Despite the fact that it was winter, Jacob was in shorts, not a goose bump in sight on his still-tan legs. Winters were mild in Valley Lake, and while no one but Jacob was wearing shorts, the sun shined bright enough that kids like Jacob who had pools in their backyards could maintain a sun-kissed look year-round. Birdie's fair skin never tanned like that no matter how much time she spent outside. If she forgot sunscreen, she burned then peeled horribly. In fact at the start of the school year, she and Hailey had bonded initially because Hailey had noticed Birdie didn't have a tan. And she'd wanted to know if Birdie had stayed inside all summer doing gymnastics. Birdie didn't do gymnastics, but it had been enough of an icebreaker for the girls to start talking.

"Hey!" Birdie waved to the boys like she was the housing development's welcoming committee.

"Isn't that Mike Hutchenson's canoe?" the older boy asked. He'd dressed more for the weather in ripped black jeans. He also wore a *Thrasher* skater T-shirt—the kind Birdie longed for, but could never find at thrift stores. He spoke like Birdie and Hailey weren't there.

"He said we could borrow it," Hailey lied.

Jacob's brother took two leaps up the stairs, walking uninvited into the girls' newly christened fort.

"You think Mike would let a couple of babies borrow his canoe?"

"Hey, they're my age," Jacob protested.

His brother smirked. "Exactly."

"Looks like you might have borrowed a canoe yourself," Birdie pointed out.

Jacob smiled like for a moment he was on Birdie's side. "She's onto us, Travis."

Travis took another step into the girls' fort like he owned it and the world, too. "It's time for you two to go home and play My Little Pony or whatever it is that girls do."

There were so many other almost-houses the boys could choose for themselves. Why were they bothering them? "You're trespassing," Birdie observed. Sure, she didn't have any real claim to the wood under her feet, but neither did these boys, Birdie could tell. They were being mean for the heck of it, and she wasn't going to stand for it.

"Trespassing?" Travis laughed.

Hailey had lied so Birdie did, too, continuing their game of pretend. "My parents own this house, so yeah." A tremendous untruth, since first of all, Birdie only had one parent, and second of all, Mama had never owned any house, and probably never would. She wasn't sure if Jacob already knew this about her or not. Probably he did, since Birdie's mother occasionally made an appearance at Valley Lake Elementary in her Clean as a Whistle uniform, but she couldn't seem to shut up. "They own all these houses, in fact," she embellished.

Hailey backed her up. "They asked us to check on them. Make sure the construction was coming along according to schedule."

Jacob tugged Travis's arm when he didn't turn. "Let's go."

It was a whopper of a story. Did Jacob actually believe her?

Travis, though, didn't seem quite as gullible. He shook off his brother and started digging through the construction debris. He pulled out a flat piece of wood and set it up to roll his skateboard over. "I bet your parents don't even know you're here. I also bet if you know what's good for you, you won't say a word if we walk off with whatever we find that's useful."

Birdie reached an arm toward Travis's skateboard. "Oh, we're making bets? I bet I can ollie this ten-stair on that board of yours." She was dying to change the subject, and plus, it kept nagging at her how she ended yesterday on her butt. She had a skateboarding code. If she crashed, fell down, or otherwise messed up, she had to immediately get back on and try again.

And while there was nothing she could do about Mrs. Hillmore's broken ice skater, she could make things right with herself and her board.

Both boys laughed.

"Come on, hand it over." Birdie motioned with her hand, begging for the board.

Hailey looked at Birdie in surprise. She was probably wondering if Birdie actually knew how to do something like that.

Birdie gave a slight nod.

Hailey's back straightened. "If she nails the landing, you go back to where you came from."

"And if she breaks her face?" Travis handed Birdie his skateboard like he couldn't wait to see her nose in a bloody splatter, her lips smacked into concrete, her eyes shoved into the other side of her head.

"We leave. We never saw you," Hailey said.

"Deal." Jacob stepped forward. He put out his hand toward Birdie.

She shook it, gripping with all her might so Jacob Powers would know that Birdie Loggerman was made of nails, not nail polish. Then she walked the skateboard as far back from the stairs as she could to give herself the longest possible runway. Suddenly, the fact that the house didn't have any walls seemed like good fortune. In her mind the unfinished wood shaped itself into an epic skate park for her to tear up.

She hopped on and the board under her feet gave her heart wings. Then seconds later, her body joined her heart, and she was flying through the air and over the stairs. She grabbed the bottom of the board and twisted to the side for effect. And as luck and Birdie's skill would have it, she landed on the dirt without falling over.

"Whoa," Jacob said.

Birdie hadn't heard the sound of awe in a long time—at least not in relation to herself.

"Deal's a deal, fellas," Hailey reminded the boys after a few seconds of stunned silence.

Silence in which Jacob Powers stared gape-jawed at Birdie like he'd never seen her before, and well, maybe he hadn't, really. Rich kids like Jacob saw Birdie's beat-up sneakers and off-brand clothes and quickly looked away.

Hailey folded her arms over her chest, and her eyes went meaningfully to the boys' canoe, like they better get to paddling or else. What she would do, Birdie wasn't sure, but to her surprise, the boys took their skateboards and climbed back into their canoe without another word.

As they paddled away, Hailey turned to Birdie with a huge smile. She put her hand in the air for a high five.

Birdie put up her own hand, and as she touched it to her friend's, she felt the world shift toward her for once instead of away. Like maybe all those lies she'd told had spun a new reality. One where she was a success instead of a screwup. Lucky instead of unlucky. Rich instead of poor. A new reality where she was the proud owner of a girls-only fort on the lake.

3

The girls paddled themselves back across the water toward home—or at least Birdie was paddling. Hailey stood in the canoe shouting and waving her arms, excited by the power of Birdie's words. "That was amazing when you said it was your house."

"I don't know," Birdie said, thinking the story would have been much more believable coming from Hailey. Hailey's parents actually had the money to own a house. And why did Birdie have to say her parents owned *all* the houses? There was something about living in Valley Lake that made her feel like she had to be so much better than she was. "I really shouldn't have made stuff up like that."

"Of course, you should've. How else would we have gotten out of that?"

Birdie let this sink in. She'd never heard someone be so cavalier about lying. Mama had told her if she ever really needed to, she could lie about her father, but that it was better to just avoid the subject if she could. If someone asked, she usually said, *He left, and I don't want to talk about it,* which most of the time was pretty much the truth.

"How come you never told me you knew how to do tricks like that on a skateboard?"

Birdie shrugged. "Guess I'm not the only one who knows how to stick a landing."

Her friend raised her arms like she'd just landed off the gymnastics vault.

Birdie stopped paddling and put her hands on the edges of the canoe. She made it rock back and forth so Hailey would wobble.

Hailey sat down fast. "I can't fall in."

"I wouldn't really shake it that hard," Birdie promised.

"Good," Hailey said, standing up again.

"Boo!" A voice behind Birdie shouted.

Hailey startled, lost her balance, and flopped into the water with a loud smack.

"Oh my god! Hailey!" Birdie shouted.

"Oops, did I scare her?" Travis laughed. The boys' canoe had been hidden in a section of the lake with a lot of reeds.

Jacob looked upset. "Can she swim?" He stared into the water where Hailey had gone under, and more importantly, where she wasn't coming up.

Birdie didn't wait to find out. The water shocked her skin like a slap. Even though January wasn't that cold in Valley Lake, the water felt to Birdie like it belonged in the Arctic.

Her hands touched and tangled into slimy things. She opened her eyes to search for Hailey, but all she saw was gunk. Lake gunk that was green and black and impossible to see through. But she thrashed and fought through the water until she felt her friend's arm and looped it into hers.

But Hailey sucked onto Birdie like an octopus. Arms and legs intertwined into Birdie's in tight grips. Hailey was pulling Birdie down with her. Birdie couldn't get free. Self-preservation instinct took over.

She kneed Hailey in the gut.

Hailey released her. Birdie's hand found the top of the canoe. Her other hand reached long toward Hailey. She grabbed her friend's hair and pulled, yanking her to the surface.

Hailey sputtered and coughed and threw her arms over the boat.

"You guys are jerks!" Birdie shouted. She watched in horror as Hailey spit and coughed over and over.

Finally, her friend caught her breath.

"At least I'm not a liar, poor girl," Travis shouted over the lake.

His words sank like shark bites into Birdie's heart. The simple truth of them stung.

She held the canoe steady as her friend climbed in, and she tried to push back the hurt. If only he'd called her something more awful, but less true. She'd always been poor, and it had never bothered her that much. But she used to live in Polkville where everyone else was, too. The desperation in Mama's whispers on the phone last night came back to her. It left her colder than the lake. If she was poor now, how poor would they be if Mama didn't have a job?

Hailey's previously perfect hair now clung to her face like seaweed slime, her clothes were dripping wet, and her fuzzy boots were ruined.

Birdie suddenly remembered the expensive leather bookbag her friend had with her. "Your bag!"

Hailey shrugged, then shivered. "Forget it."

But Birdie dived back into the thick, murky water to look for it. There were a ton of plants. And as she swam down toward the lake's bottom, she realized its depth. She shot up to the surface. Then she tried again, diving back under.

"Forget it, seriously," Hailey yelled.

But it was such a nice bag.

"My mom is going to kill me," Hailey said when Birdie climbed back into the canoe, also soaking wet and cold.

Buying a new bookbag just five months into the school year would make Birdie's mom frantic. "My mom would kill me if I lost my bag, too."

"She won't care about that."

Oh, of course. Hailey's parents had the money to replace things—even expensive things.

"I'm not supposed to go across the lake."

"You aren't?"

Hailey shook her head. "Mom thinks I'll drown."

"Oh." Well, her friend *had* almost drowned. "You can't swim?"

Hailey shook her head. "Not really."

"Why didn't your mom get you swimming lessons?" Even Birdie's mama had found the money so Birdie could learn.

"I do gymnastics every day."

Hailey didn't just take gymnastics classes on Saturday mornings like the other girls. She went every day after school, too. Still, it seemed crazy. Hailey lived on a lake. How did she not know how to swim?

"What will you say?" Birdie asked.

"Anything but the truth."

Birdie didn't have much reason in this instance to lie to her mama. Mama had never said she couldn't go across the lake. But even if she did have a reason, she wouldn't. She couldn't. It was just her and Mama, and that made them close.

Hailey paused as if to think. "I just have to come up

with an explanation. A good reason for why I look like a swamp rat and smell like a dead fish. The perfect lie to get myself out of this mess."

Birdie thought, too. "What if you tell her there was a giant sinkhole filled with lake water? And you were walking along and didn't see it?"

Hailey cocked her eyebrow and stared at Birdie a long beat. "Okay, I've got it. Mom is at Pilates. Dad is at work. I can sneak back into my house, dry off and change clothes, and she'll never know anything happened."

"Genius!"

The plan in place, the girls paddled to shore, returned the canoe, and ran home dripping mad. Mad to be outsmarted. Mad not to have the last word or trick. Madder still when they realized that inside Hailey's bag at the bottom of the lake was the key they needed to get inside Hailey's house.

4

The girls walked from window to window, their wet pants sticking uncomfortably to their legs, looking for one that was unlocked. "Nothing like trying to break into your own house," Hailey said.

"Found one!" Birdie called.

"Oh, man, are you kidding me?" Hailey seemed disappointed.

"What?"

Her friend bit her lip. "This is my parents' room."

"So? They're not here. Give me your foot, I'll lift you up."

Hailey looked unsure. Her head turned to the

treehouse in the backyard—the beautiful one, hand-crafted by her dad. The one they'd hung out in everyday after school since they'd become friends at the beginning of the school year. The one Hailey's mother said they were no longer allowed inside. "Mom never lets me in her room."

"Really?" Birdie couldn't imagine not being allowed into her own mother's room. But then Birdie and Mama's tiny apartment was only two bedrooms. Maybe when you had tons of space like the Kirklands, you could more easily say certain rooms were off-limits. Birdie tried to think. There was a trapdoor in the treehouse. Last she saw, inside it was the game Taboo, some snacks, and a blanket. "Unless you have a change of clothes hidden in the treehouse, I don't think you have a choice." They'd checked most of the other windows already, and they were all locked.

"That would have been such a good idea. But I don't." Hailey took off her wet shoes and socks so she wouldn't track mud and lake water in her parents' bedroom, then put her foot into Birdie's outstretched hand. She threw herself over the window ledge and tumbled inside.

"You okay?" Birdie asked.

Instead of answering, Hailey leaned out the window and grabbed Birdie in a long hug. A hug that seemed to acknowledge that Hailey had maybe almost died and that Birdie had saved her.

"You're okay," Birdie said.

"Yeah." Hailey released her. "I'm good. I'm going to go shower."

And Birdie got out of there before Hailey's parents could arrive.

The next day, she wanted to find out if the plan had worked—if Hailey had been able to get herself cleaned up and changed before she got caught. Had Mrs. Kirkland noticed Hailey was wearing a different outfit than she had been earlier in the day? Hailey's mom was probably the type to pay attention to details like that.

Birdie was about to leave to catch the bus to school where she hoped to find out the answers to these burning questions when Mama offered to give her a ride. Normally, Mama didn't have time to drive Birdie to school. Normally, Mama would be wearing her black maid's uniform with Clean as a Whistle stitched into the fabric—instead of slacks and a too-bright orange sweater featuring an enormous sunflower.

"Don't you have to be at the Dupreys' by eight?" Birdie asked, hoping against hope that she'd been wrong, and Mama hadn't been fired after all.

"No, not today," Mama said. "I have to run a few errands and Valley Lake is on the way."

Valley Lake Elementary was on a long road with a lot of businesses—pharmacies, grocery stores, dentists' offices. It was impossible to narrow down what kind of errand her mother might need to run. But Birdie had a bad feeling all these errands had to do with Mama needing to find a new job. "Is everything okay?" She knew it wasn't, but she had to ask. "Did you get in trouble with Clean as a Whistle?"

Mama nodded.

Birdie's stomach dropped. "Can I help?"

"Thank you, but I don't think so," Mama said.

But Birdie had to, so when Mama wasn't looking, she stuck her hand into Mama's purse and felt around until she landed on some business cards. Each one had a picture of a tiny mop next to the words: *Janey Loggerman, Maid Services,* along with Mama's phone number.

There were five cards in the pile. Birdie would choose wisely. She'd give each of them to the richest kids in her grade. Kids like Hailey and Jacob Powers.

Jacob and his brother had been so mean. Jacob owed her.

But as soon as she saw Jacob at school, her stomach flew out from under her like her board on a flubbed trick. It was on the tip of her tongue to tell him off, that he and his brother were totally out of line yesterday, but when he turned his dark eyes on her, she found herself saying instead, "Can you give this to your parents? My aunt is looking for a job." The lie slid out of her mouth warm and comfortable as a buttered biscuit. "Please," she begged when Jacob hesitated. "She's new to town—her husband left her, and she could really use the money."

Jacob took the card. "Okay. I'll ask."

It was true that Aunt Laura's husband had left her, but the rest was not. Aunt Laura was a waitress in Polkville where she lived with Birdie's cousin, Kellog. Why couldn't she admit it was her own mama looking for a job?

She promised herself she wouldn't lie anymore. But when she handed the next of Mama's business cards to Aiden Fuller, her tongue wagged the same tale.

It happened again when she asked Samiya Naidu, and again when she asked Lily Michaels. Hailey had acted like lying was no big deal, but by the time Birdie got to the cafeteria for lunch, the lies had eaten her appetite. She was usually starving by now, but today she didn't care that she'd be late for turkey and mashed potatoes with gravy—her favorite school lunch.

Hailey had brought lunch from home so she was already sitting at the sixth-grade lunch table. Instead of waiting in the long line for school lunch, Birdie joined her friend. Finally, someone she didn't have to lie to. Finally, someone she could count on to help. "Can you ask your mom if—"

"I'm sorry, but I'm not allowed to talk to you anymore," Hailey interrupted. She scooted down the bench a few inches.

"What?" Birdie asked. She didn't understand.

"I'm sorry. My mom won't let me." Hailey put her hand in front of her mouth and lowered her voice as if they were in the library. "We'll have to talk later when no one's looking. My mom found my wet clothes. I had to tell her about the lake."

"Okay." Birdie paused, confused. "But that wasn't my fault." Sure, she'd helped borrow a canoe that wasn't hers and made up some stuff, but she hadn't caused Hailey to fall in the lake. And it definitely wasn't her fault that Hailey didn't know how to swim.

"I know," Hailey said. "But my mom thinks it is."

"Why would she think that?" Birdie's voice rose and the other girls at the table turned to stare.

"You know . . . ," Hailey said vaguely, smoothing her jean skirt over her legs like it was wrinkled, which it wasn't. She paused as if Birdie could fill in the rest.

"No, I don't know." Birdie folded her arms over her chest.

"Because of where you live."

Birdie felt her cheeks heat up.

"She says it's the wrong side of town," Hailey explained. "She thinks you're a bad influence even though I told her that you weren't. I told her you helped me, but she wouldn't listen. You know how my mom is." She shrugged like she didn't know how else to explain it.

Birdie wanted to shout that there was no wrong side of town, but she could tell by the other girls' pitying faces that this time lying wasn't going to save her. They all already knew the truth.

"She's always trying to control my life," Hailey complained. "She's crazy."

Birdie hadn't realized that where she lived was so bad that Hailey's mom would blame her for something she hadn't done. Because there wasn't anything she could do about where she lived. And Birdie was the sort of girl who did things. Always with passion, often without thinking.

Face burning, she did something without thinking now. "She's more than crazy. She's a—" And out popped a word as straight-edged and sharp as Hailey's haircut. A word you couldn't take back.

A word a lot more wrong than any side of town.

5

"Why would you say a thing like that?" Mrs. Alverez asked her. Birdie had been sent to the assistant principal's office, because the lunch lady had overheard the razor-sharp word she'd called Hailey's mom.

"But we weren't in class," Birdie offered up in her defense, hoping that lunchtime was off the record. She didn't want to be guilty. She didn't want to have to explain that the actual wrong here wasn't her or the side of town she lived on, but Hailey's mom.

"You were on school property." Mrs. Alvarez motioned to a window, which overlooked the cafeteria. "And even if you hadn't been, is that a thing you ought to say?" Mrs. Alverez leaned her hefty frame across the desk in case Birdie didn't understand that assistant principals didn't put up with any nonsense.

"No," Birdie said, suddenly aware she might be severely punished. At her old school in Polkville, actions were more likely than words to get you into trouble.

"Next time if you're angry, I want you to count to ten before you say anything. Can you do that for me?"

"Yes," Birdie agreed, though this sort of thing wasn't her strength.

"If you learn to think before you speak, your life will be better . . . *richer,* in the ways that matter most," Mrs. Alverez said as if she could see through Birdie's used clothes and dirty sneakers to the heart of the problem. But all Birdie could think was if she were actually richer, as in not poor, this whole thing never would have happened.

"Relationships are life's greatest treasure," Mrs. Alverez went on. "Our friends are a gift. We have to hold them close."

"I'm sorry. I won't even think that awful word. I promise." This seemed the safest way to make sure it didn't find its way off her tongue again.

Mrs. Alverez nodded, firm like a handshake. "I won't see you here again then?"

Birdie agreed, and she was dismissed without further punishment. Relieved, she skipped to class and even did a cartwheel in the middle of the empty hallway.

Only later Birdie understood she'd been foolish to celebrate, because for the rest of the day none of her friends would talk to her. Birdie was grateful when school let out, and she could go straight home. When she reached Woodcroft Apartments and the overgrown grass outside unit 208, she climbed up onto the broken trampoline and sat. There, she spent some time fiddling with the loose springs, and thinking about right versus wrong.

She'd been wrong to call Hailey's mother the very bad word. She'd been angry, and she'd reacted—she'd been doing this a lot lately. But she didn't think her *neighborhood* was wrong. It hadn't done anything unjust—at least not as far as she knew. Hailey had never even been to Birdie's apartment, so how did her mother know it was so bad?

Still, she tried to assess Woodcroft Apartments the way Hailey's mother might. As far as exteriors went, the weeds tickled the tops of your ankles when you walked. Instead of nice flowers, like she'd seen at Hailey's house, Woodcroft had colorful chip bags (Fritos, Doritos, Lay's) tumbling across the parking lot like confetti, the occasional rolling soda can and wind-whipped Reese's Peanut Butter Cups wrappers. Nicer apartment complexes came with playgrounds or pools, but at Woodcroft kids played basketball in the parking lot using a trash can as a goal and dodging cars backing out as they ran.

The building itself featured nearly matching units in various shades of brown, as if they'd been repainted, but someone had gotten the original color slightly wrong each time. There was that word she didn't like again. *Wrong.* Could a *neighborhood* be wrong? A *building*? A *place*?

Or wasn't it only *people* who could do wrong?

People like Hailey's mom who obviously thought being poor made you to blame.

Not that Birdie was blameless. She'd messed up calling Hailey's mother that word, and she'd messed up big-time at Mrs. Hillmore's house. She knew she had. She'd been going with Mama to the houses where she cleaned since she was small, because Mama couldn't afford a babysitter. And she'd been told a million times to be careful. She knew better than to stand on a skateboard inside a house. Of course she did.

She just got so freaking mad sometimes.

Mama came down the stairs from their apartment and stood in front of Birdie. She wore a dress that looked like it came from another decade. It had colors as blindingly bright as the sun. Yellows swirled up with reds in a pattern that made Birdie a little dizzy. As much as she hated Mama's black Clean as a Whistle maid's uniform, Birdie would give anything to see her in it now.

"Are you okay?" Mama asked Birdie.

She shrugged.

"When you come home from school, you ought to let me know you're here before you play outside. Otherwise I worry," Mama said.

Birdie nodded.

"I heard you had a horrible day."

This meant that Birdie's trip to Mrs. Alverez's office had not been as scot-free as she'd assumed. That in addition to the punishment of having Hailey and the rest of the girls ignore her at lunch, Mrs. Alverez had called her mother.

"Hailey's mom is mean as a snake. She's never liked me and for no good reason."

Mama nodded. "Maybe so. But two wrongs don't make a right. And you can't let that kind of thing mess you up in school." Mama climbed up onto the trampoline, avoiding the giant rip torn down the left side, her dress bunching up around her, until she sat beside Birdie. She put her arm over Birdie's shoulders, and Birdie leaned in and inhaled. Mama smelled like peanut butter and semi-sweet chocolate.

"You making buckeyes?"

Mama nodded. "You can come inside and help me dip some." The peanut butter balls had to get covered in the melted chocolate.

"Did you make them for me?"

"I did," Mama said.

It was so nice it made Birdie's throat swell up. "Why? I got in trouble at school. I thought you'd be mad at me." Seeing as how Birdie had lost Mama her job, Birdie wouldn't blame her if she was mad at her for the rest of her life.

"No, I'm not mad. I understand it's difficult for you to fit in with a lot of the kids here. I feel bad about that. I keep hoping another kid your age will move to Woodcroft so you can get a new friend."

Most of the kids at Woodcroft were either much older than her or way younger. Dre-Mon in fifth grade was the closest to her age, but he ate crickets for fun. But not having kids her age at Woodcroft wasn't really the problem. There were other kids at school. Most of them had more money than her, sure, but not everyone was as rich as Hailey, and probably not everyone had a mom as stuck-up as Mrs. Kirkland.

"It's not your fault, Mama. I know better. It's just—I don't want a new friend. I want Hailey." As rich as Hailey was, she never looked at Birdie like she was worthless. But Mrs. Kirkland had. And now that she had made it clear that Birdie wasn't good enough, Birdie didn't think she was either.

Mama got off the trampoline and put out her hand. "Come on, then. Let's go make some buckeyes."

Birdie didn't deserve it after all the trouble she'd caused. Especially since all she had thought about lately was how rich she wanted to be—right when they were poorer than ever. She owed it to Mama to be grateful, humble, and kind. She sucked in a deep breath of fresh sunshiny air and followed Mama inside.

6

Birdie had Mrs. Fitzgerald's math class last period. She had her homework all ready to turn in, and she should've been proud that she'd figured out the correct answers to all her word problems. But she wasn't.

Instead of listening to Mrs. Fitzgerald's lesson, she traced a line in her notebook. She drew the line over and over again until her pencil popped a hole through the paper. She tore out the ruined sheet and the sheet underneath it—which was also ruined, and just like that her notebook was clean again.

It was an entirely fixable problem to have put a hole in a sheet of paper. A hole in a wall on the other hand was harder to fix. A glass ice skater broken into a million pieces—well, forget it.

But somehow, she had to right the wrongs.

Let's see. If she sold buckeye candy balls, each for twenty-five cents, how many would she have to sell to make, oh say, a hundred dollars? She did the math and discovered she would have to sell four hundred. Each recipe made sixty buckeyes, so she would need to make seven batches.

That was an awful lot of candy.

Maybe she should charge more. But would anyone pay fifty cents for one tiny bite of candy? She wasn't sure. She also wasn't sure how much all the supplies would cost—the peanut butter, chocolate, sugar, and butter she would need. They weren't free. So, she'd have to subtract that cost from her profits, and then she'd have to find a stadium full of rich kids to purchase it all. It didn't sound easy, but Birdie was up for the challenge.

When she got home from school, she found her mother at the kitchen table. "Can we go to the grocery store?" she asked before she even set down her backpack.

"Why? I just went the other day. What do you need?" Mama looked up from a calculator where she was punching in numbers. Birdie also noticed Mama was surrounded by papers that looked like bills.

"I wanted to get some supplies to make some more buckeyes."

"We still have some in the fridge."

"I know. But I want to make more."

"I'm sorry, sweetheart. I don't think we'll be buying anything we don't absolutely need anytime soon. You'll have to enjoy what we have while it lasts."

"Oh." Birdie got some crackers and some cheese for a snack and sat down next to Mama. "What are you doing?"

"Nothing you should concern yourself with." Mama tried to shield the papers from Birdie's view.

"Please, can I help?" Birdie begged. "I want to know how much everything costs."

"You're too young to worry yourself with bills. You've got the rest of your life for that."

"I'm not too young. We studied budgets last year in math. I had a pretend paycheck, rent to pay, groceries to buy—an electric bill and everything."

Mama looked amused. "Did you, now?"

"I did. And I got an A-plus on that assignment, I'll have you know. So, maybe I can help."

"I appreciate it, sweetie. I really do, but I can handle this myself." Mama smiled and pushed what she'd been working on under a newspaper. "Do you want to watch some TV with me?"

"Okay."

But later when Mama went into the bathroom, Birdie slid the newspaper over so she could see. Mama had made out a list of expenses for the month. Instead of writing out the words, she'd drawn a little picture next to a number: a house for rent, a lamp for energy, a car for gas, a banana for food. The pictures were cute—almost funny. But the amount of money they needed was no joke.

Birdie retyped the numbers into the calculator to check her mother's math, and indeed the total was almost eight hundred dollars. There was no way Birdie could sell that much candy. Birdie picked up a bill and noticed the price for trash pickup.

Fifty-five dollars?

That was crazy. She couldn't let Mama pay that anymore. All she had to do was ask Jessie if he would put their trash in his truck when he went to the dump. Their proud Puerto Rican neighbor was known at Woodcroft Apartments as something of a Good Samaritan. He was the kind of person you could ask if you needed help changing a tire or replacing a light bulb. She'd gone to the dump with him once, because she wanted to ride in his pickup truck. It had been her lucky day, because she'd found the trampoline there. Jessie had fixed the broken springs, and it had lasted almost the whole summer before some jerk had ripped a hole straight through the middle.

When Mama came out of the bathroom, Birdie was back on the sofa in front of the TV like she'd never left. "Do we pay for trash pickup?" Birdie asked like she didn't know the answer.

"Yes," Mama said. "Why?"

"Jessie takes his bags to the dump himself. I bet he wouldn't mind taking ours, too."

"That's a great idea," Mama said, ruffling Birdie's hair. "Jessie is such a nice guy. It's amazing how he helps everyone around here."

"I'll go ask him right now. I'll give him the rest of the buckeye candies to thank him when he says yes. Leave it to me, Mama. This is one bill we'll never have to pay again."

_7_

Jessie said it would be no problem to take Birdie and Mama's trash with his own, and he even refused to let Birdie give him anything for it. She didn't quite understand why someone would want to do chores for other people if they weren't getting paid—or getting candy at least. But she was relieved the problem was solved.

The next afternoon in history class, Mr. Gladwell passed around the field trip permission slips for going to the Biltmore Estate, while lecturing them on proper behavior on the bus and asking for volunteer parents to help chaperone. For a brief second, Birdie got excited. Since Mama didn't have to go to work, maybe she could come on the field trip, too. All the other kids' moms always got to come, but Birdie's never had. But when Birdie read the permission slip, her heart sank.

Forty dollars.

There was no way in the world she was getting forty dollars to go on a field trip. Mr. Gladwell had talked about the trip to the Biltmore Estate for weeks. You'd think he'd have thought to mention it cost money.

He probably didn't mention it because most kids' parents had no problem shelling out money for an educational trip. Most kids didn't have to worry about how they would pay for rent or food, never mind a few extra bucks for admission to a really cool mansion. She sank down in her seat. She'd probably be the only kid left behind.

After class she went up to Mr. Gladwell and handed back her permission slip. "I won't be able to go." She stood tall and firm. She'd accepted her fate.

He looked alarmed. "Why not?"

"Forty dollars is a lot of money for some people," she explained. Out of the corner of her eye she noticed Lily Michaels, her perfectly sun-kissed arms stacking and restacking her books. She was listening.

"Are you an adult already?" Mr. Gladwell asked, not taking the form back.

"No."

He smiled. "Then it's only twenty dollars."

"Oh." Birdie read the sheet again—this time more carefully. Adult admission forty dollars, children half off.

Mortifyingly, Lily was still there pretending to pack up. Her blond hair bobbed over a gorgeous navy dress with sparkly-silver buttons. A dress that looked like it cost a small fortune. Her matching silver ballet flats inched closer to Birdie and her conversation.

It was on the tip of Birdie's tongue to tell Lily to mind her own business. She also had an overwhelming urge to reach over and pluck off one of Lily's sparkly-silver buttons, to pop it right from her dress, but since Mr. Gladwell stood watch, by some miracle, she resisted.

Instead she pushed the sheet back in Mr. Gladwell's direction. "It doesn't matter. I don't have twenty dollars either."

Mr. Gladwell smiled even bigger, and then he winked at her. "Just get your parent to sign the form, and I'll take care of the rest."

There was a part of her that didn't want charity. But another part of her that desperately wanted to see a great big mansion—the largest one in the United States—and an even bigger part that wanted this conversation to be over. So, she said, "Okay," and put the sheet into her bookbag.

She wasn't looking forward to showing the form to Mama. Mama wouldn't like Mr. Gladwell paying just for Birdie. On the other hand, if he paid for the whole class then that might be okay. No, she didn't want to lie. She really didn't. But how else would she get to go on the trip?

8

On Monday, she sat in what was now her usual spot at lunch—the very end of the sixth-grade table, three feet from the other kids. But Lily Michaels came and closed the space. She sat right beside Birdie and proceeded to pray.

Yes, pray.

Head bowed, eyes closed, hands clasped together. After a long and uncomfortable few minutes, Birdie had to interrupt. "What are you doing?"

"I'm praying for you," Lily said.

Birdie felt a surge of anger. Was she making fun of her?

Lily continued, "I overheard you talking to Mr. Gladwell last week."

"You shouldn't have been listening," Birdie snapped.

"I know, I'm sorry." Lily lowered her eyes. "I couldn't help it."

Birdie softened. She could understand impulses and the inability to stop them. "What were you praying for . . . exactly?"

"For you to get money, of course."

Birdie was shocked. She wasn't religious, so she didn't know how it worked. "You can pray for that? You can pray to *get* stuff?"

"Sure," Lily said. "You can pray for whatever you want. But it's better if you're praying for someone else—especially if you're asking for material possessions or money."

Huh. This was interesting. "Does it work?" Birdie asked.

"Oh, yes," Lily said, her voice serious. "Prayer is powerful."

Birdie wondered when she could expect to get the money that Lily had prayed for her to have. "I could use it soon. If you wouldn't mind telling Him." She was thinking about the rent due in two days.

"Sure." Lily smiled. "I'll let Him know. If you want, you can come to church with me on Sunday." She paused. "It might help you get on His good side."

Birdie had always been curious about church. Hailey went occasionally, and when she did, she and Lily talked about it on Mondays. So, like gymnastics, it felt like just another thing Birdie was left out of on the weekends. But Sunday would be too late since the rent was due Wednesday. And anyway, Birdie had noticed that Mama was nearly out of gas. Birdie might not have a way to get to church. "Is there a way I can get on His good side *sooner*?"

"You could pray," Lily suggested.

Samiya Naidu had been watching their conversation with interest. Birdie noted a slight eye roll, like Samiya didn't think praying for money was going to work. Samiya was Indian, and she'd shared about being a Hindu last year as part of a cultural diversity unit. Maybe Hindus didn't believe you could pray for money.

It seemed pretty far-fetched to Birdie, too, but she was desperate. "Okay, thanks."

She opened her mouth to ask Lily if maybe she could get a ride with her to church—even though rent was due Wednesday, maybe they could be a little late, but Lily got up and joined Hailey who was sitting at the other end of the table.

Birdie got the distinct impression that she wasn't exactly being welcomed back into the fold—that instead she was some kind of pity project—but she didn't have time to waste worrying about it.

Birdie immediately clapped her hands together in prayer.

She prayed every moment she could. She prayed for one thing. Money for Mama. And Lily had said if she prayed for someone else, it would work.

So, Birdie prayed. And when it came to praying for something, Birdie went all in. She didn't just pray for rent money, or money for gas or money to fix Mrs. Hillmore's living room wall and to buy her another ice skater. Oh no, she prayed for piles of money. Crazy money. Enough that Mama never had to work again.

Because Birdie didn't want Mama to have to clean houses anymore for stuck-up rich folks like Hailey's mom or even Mrs. Hillmore, who couldn't forgive one little accident. Mama deserved a better life than this one full of worry.

And Birdie intended to get it for her.

But rent day came and went with no sign that anyone was listening to her pleas. She'd even gotten down on her knees beside her bed and prayed every night before she went to sleep. She'd prayed at mealtimes and in between mealtimes. She'd prayed so much that her palms got sweaty from pressing her hands together so tight.

Surely, it was just a matter of time.

But the day after rent day came and went as well. And then Friday and then Saturday, until finally it was Sunday.

And still no money.

Nevertheless, she was still busy praying—as best as she knew how. No money had fallen from the sky to save them, so her work was not done.

"Everything okay? You're awfully quiet today," Mama said as they pulled into Woodcroft's parking lot.

Birdie watched the gas gauge now directly over the E. They had used their last drops to get Mama a newspaper so she could look for jobs. Birdie couldn't tell Mama her worries, so she said, "Nothing's wrong. I'm fine."

But she was far from it. The apartment's manager, a Black lady named Ronda King, stood in front of her and Mama's apartment waving an envelope. "Hello!" she called when she saw them get out of the car.

"Coming!" Mama called, and she rushed to the door—probably to stop Ronda from yelling across the parking lot.

"You forgot to pay your rent this month," Ronda sing-songed as they approached. Her dark arm swung the envelope back and forth like she was directing an orchestra.

"Thank you." Mama nodded, opening her purse. She fished for her key.

But Ronda blocked the door. "You can pay me now, and we'll be all settled."

"It's Sunday," Mama said.

"They tell me to come out exactly five days after rent is due no matter what day of the week it is. And it has been five days for you." She tapped Mama's shoulder with the envelope like Mama had been a disobedient puppy.

Mama took the letter and side-stepped Ronda to get the key in the door. "I'm sure we're not the first people in this large complex to be a bit late with the rent."

"You're not. Which is why the owner is very well versed in the eviction process."

This was not what Birdie had been expecting. She looked at the sky. What the heck, God?

Mama ignored her, and finally got the door open. Ronda pushed her nose in as if Mama were hiding a game show–size check right there in the living room. Birdie was hopeful, too.

But no.

Everything was as they'd left it. "Thank you again," Mama said, closing the door in Ronda's face.

Birdie had given God a firm deadline, and it had more than passed. What were they going to do? Without gas money, even sleeping at the skate park wasn't an option. Why did some people have so much and some people so little?

Mama pulled off her shoes and lay down on the

sofa. She flopped her arm over her eyes and heaved the world's most exasperated sigh. The kind of sigh that should make the angels weep. A sigh that should have brought gold-coined tears down from the heavens.

But it didn't, and Birdie couldn't stand to watch. So, she slipped off to her bedroom to flop her own arm over her own eyes and heave her own exasperated sigh. Eventually, she fell asleep and dreamed a dream. And in it, the angels were laughing.

9

The next day at school, Birdie decided she was done with the three-foot space at lunchtime. She was going to plop herself down right next to Lily even if it meant being within saying-sorry distance of Hailey. Maybe, just maybe, if she got up enough nerve she would apologize.

But by the time Birdie got her lunch tray, Lily and the girls were already seated. And as expected, on one side of Lily was Hailey, but on the other was something unexpected: a giant garbage bag.

"Birdie!" Lily waved her over.

The garbage bag was black, so Birdie couldn't see what was inside, but it was definitely full of something.

It was sitting on the seat where a person should sit—not far in fact from Birdie's usual seat. Her guard flew up. She eyed the fifth-grade table to see if she could sit next to Dre-Mon. She didn't even care if she had to watch him eat crickets. But he was jammed in tight with a bunch of boys she didn't know.

Lily waved at her again.

Birdie approached the table cautiously, as she might a pack of wild dogs. She pointed. "What's that?"

"I brought you some stuff." Lily's voice was over-excited, and she bounced on her seat. "Come see."

Birdie stepped a tad closer. She dared to balance her lunch tray on the end of her usual spot.

Lily began to pull things out of the trash bag. Birdie recognized some of the items as Lily's clothes. She spotted the pretty navy dress with sparkly-silver buttons that Lily had worn just last week.

Lily held up a gray sweater to her chest. "I love this one. And I thought it would match your sneakers."

Birdie glanced down at her feet. Was Lily joking? It was hard to tell.

She remained standing, her tray balanced on the end of the table, unable to decide if she should be offended. She was distracted by the navy dress peeking out of the bag.

As if she'd read her mind, Lily chose the dress to pull out next. "I saw how much you liked this, and I"— Lily paused as if she didn't know quite how to put it.

Hailey and the other girls leaned in—"I thought you should have it." Lily thrust the navy dress toward Birdie.

"I couldn't," Birdie said, though she'd coveted Lily's dress so deeply she'd imagined stealing a button.

"I insist."

"Okay, thanks," Birdie found herself saying. She hooked the dress over her arm and sat down next to the giant garbage bag. She didn't know what had gotten into her. She didn't usually even like dresses—but maybe that was because the only one she owned she'd worn to her grandmother's funeral.

"Please take the whole bag," Lily gushed. "I brought it all for you."

Hailey had been watching the whole time, and now she spoke to Birdie in the same sympathetic voice, as if Birdie were sick in the hospital. "If you ever need anything . . . you know, whatever, I want you to ask me, okay?"

Birdie nodded and shoved a particularly large forkful of mashed potatoes into her mouth so she wouldn't have to say anything.

But Lily and Hailey were done. They'd turned away, and the girls were already chatting about something that had happened at gymnastics practice on Saturday.

After lunch Birdie found herself lugging the giant garbage bag of Lily's clothes down the hallway. She went to her cubby and tried to stuff it all inside, but there was no way it would fit. Lily had given her more clothes than Birdie probably had in her entire closet. Plus, Birdie's skateboard was already hogging up all the space. It was against the rules to have her skateboard out of her cubby, and considering her past experience wrecking things with it, this was probably a wise rule.

So, Birdie had to lug the garbage bag to each of her classes. She even had to set it right next to Hailey in Mrs. Fitzgerald's class, and Hailey kept looking over at Birdie like she wanted to say something—probably again in that same sympathetic, talking-to-a-dying-person voice, but Birdie couldn't stand to hear it. Instead she wanted to disappear. Especially when she dragged the garbage bag onto the school bus and had to listen to all the heckling. "What you got there, bag lady?" Aiden Fuller asked. She tried to block it out, but it was hard not to take the *bag lady* name to heart. If she wasn't one already, it seemed she might be soon.

When she got home from school, Mama asked her how her day went before turning her eyes away from the newspaper she was reading.

"Fine, and please don't ask me anything else—not one word about this bag," Birdie said.

Mama looked up, and her eyes widened at the sight of the giant garbage bag. Birdie shook her head, silently insisting she wasn't going to talk about it. And she didn't say another word, not even when Mama looked hurt and disappointed. Birdie imagined kids all over the country saying only *fine* to their parents about their day at school, and the parents wondering why their kids were such jerks.

Birdie didn't mean to be a jerk, but school was a mortifying place—a place where you could be seconds away from a horrible forever nickname like *bag lady*. There were just things that happened at school that once you escaped, you never wanted to think about again.

So, she lugged the trash bag to her room without explanation. And she immediately changed out of her T-shirt and jeans like they were crawling with lice and shame and slipped on Lily's pretty navy dress. Only it didn't *slip on* at all. It got stuck around her shoulders, and her long hair got all tangled up in it. She struggled and panicked and couldn't breathe, until finally, she managed to squirm out of it before it smothered her to death. She sucked in deep dying-person breaths of air. Then she tried again, pulling the dress over her feet. But she couldn't get it past her rear end.

Birdie stared at herself in the mirror. She was just shaped differently than Lily. She could see how Lily might have *thought* her clothes would fit. They were around the same height after all. But Birdie was broader shouldered and had bigger hip bones. The dress simply wasn't her size. None of the clothes in the bag were her size, she realized after she tried on the gray sweater that Lily thought would match her sneakers. It didn't even cover her belly button. Although she wasn't entirely sure if it was supposed to. Lily was the sort of girl who might wear a half sweater.

But Birdie wasn't.

None of this stuff was anything she wanted to wear, which was a crying shame because she could only imagine how much money it must have cost.

She put on a fresh T-shirt from her own closet and the same jeans she'd worn to school and located a pair of scissors. Then she sniped off a silver button from the navy dress that had tried to smother her and tucked it into her pocket.

Such incredible embarrassment, and all she'd gotten was a sparkly button.

Oh well. At least she hadn't been impulsive enough to steal it.

10

Every day that week, Birdie carried the sparkly button around in her pocket. When the kids at school called her bag lady, she took it out to remind herself that she wouldn't be poor forever. Soon her prayers would be answered. Lily said she had to have faith. So, she tried to believe that God would come through for her and Mama. He had to.

The following weekend they got a surprise visit from cousin Kellog and Aunt Laura. Mama checked the peephole in the door before she let them in, certain it was Ronda come to harass them for the rent check again.

Mama smoothed her hand over her unbrushed hair and looked despairingly down at her sweatpants, before throwing open the door with a sigh. "If I'd known you were coming, I would have worn something nicer, maybe put on some makeup."

But as usual Aunt Laura had on enough for the both of them. Aunt Laura's hair was hot-rolled and sprayed to perfection, and she had on so much eyeshadow that if she were onstage, the back row wouldn't miss a blink. She'd been in pageants as a kid, and the big look had stuck.

Aunt Laura gave Mama a hug and insisted, "We're family, and we understand you're going through a tough time. I tried your phone, but well, it doesn't matter. We're here now."

Was Mama already out of minutes? This was bad. It meant no one could even call her to offer her a job.

Her cousin Kellog had his skateboard with him, and he used his free arm to punch Birdie in the shoulder. "Good to see you, Nailsy."

Birdie's heart warmed. Nailsy was the kind of nickname you hoped stuck. Kellog appreciated her tough as nails, daredevil nature. Everyone else made being impulsive seem like a bad thing.

"You kids go outside while Aunt Janey and I catch up," Aunt Laura instructed.

"Can't you drive us to the skate park?" Birdie asked. She really wanted to go, and this was her chance since Aunt Laura had a car with gas in it.

"Not now," Mama said. "You can skate in the parking lot."

Birdie knew better than to complain. She started out the door, but Aunt Laura stopped her.

"Wear a hat. The sun shines even in winter." Aunt Laura thought wrinkles were life's true irreversible tragedies—as if the pound of makeup she wore couldn't make a two-hundred-year-old woman look lively.

Birdie grabbed her skateboard, and a cap Mama had gotten for free for donating blood. The hat said Blood Donors Are Quiet Heroes across the top, and it had a cartoon drop of blood with legs and a smile.

It was the kind of thing the kids at school might find a reason to make fun of, but Kellog's own hat said Tubby's Ribs and Steaks and had a cow stitched into the fabric, so she was in good company. Tubby's was the restaurant where Aunt Laura worked as a waitress.

Kellog took off out the door like he didn't care what hats they wore or where they skated as long as they were on an adventure. He skated through the parking lot and then around the apartment complex.

Birdie followed. Being taller, she had longer legs. And she caught up easily. But when she did, she didn't pass Kellog like she knew she could to prove she was faster. Instead, she skated along beside him, glad to have a friend again, and one who was so much like her.

They skated together until they got to a busy road that Birdie didn't normally cross. "Come on," Kellog said, picking up his board and dashing across the four-lane highway before Birdie could stop him.

Birdie ran after him, even though she knew Mama wouldn't want them to leave Woodcroft. "Where are you going?" she asked when she caught up.

"I want to find a pool," Kellog confessed. They were safely to the other side of the highway—the one that separated the wrong side of town from the right—or the rich anyway.

"A pool?" Birdie asked, because they hadn't brought their suits, and anyway, it was too cold for swimming.

"Some people empty their pools in the winter, and they're awesome to skate in." Kellog raised his eyebrows twice.

"Wow, that's a good idea." She'd been dying to go to the skate park, and Kellog had figured out a way for them to make their own.

"I saw these kids doing it on YouTube, and I got to thinking about all these rich people in Valley Lake. They gotta have pools, right?"

"They do have pools," Birdie said, because all the clients Mama used to work for did, and so did Lily, Jacob, and a bunch of other kids from school. "But we can't go waltzing into people's backyards." Though she wanted to.

"We're not going to do some dorky dance. We're going to skate." Kellog grinned, dropping his board onto the smooth-as-silk, wide street and zigzagging across it.

They were in Evercrest, Mrs. Hillmore's neighborhood. All the houses with bright green lawns, freshly mowed and watered. Grass that looked so perfect it had to be a lie. They passed Mrs. Hillmore's house, and Birdie sped up. She knew Mrs. Hillmore had an empty pool, but she didn't tell Kellog this.

Kellog pointed. "That one has cars in the driveway. We have to pick one where no one's home."

"I guess we can always leave if someone yells at us," Birdie reasoned, because while she felt a little swallowed on the wide streets in Mrs. Hillmore's neighborhood without Mama, how often did she get to see Kellog? They deserved to make the most of it.

Suddenly, she remembered a house she'd overheard Mrs. Kirkland complaining about a few months back. The *eyesore of Evercrest*. "I know of a house no one lives in."

"Oh yeah?"

"Yeah." Birdie pointed to a house on Lakeshore Drive with no cars at the end of a cul-de-sac. It was a gray house with red shutters hidden by trees, and it stuck out as different, because the yard looked unkept—the grass a lot less green. There was a painted wooden sign nailed to a tree in the front yard that said: Lake House Investments, Huge Returns.

They ran over and peeked in the windows. "This is lucky!" Kellog said.

Inside, the house was empty. No furniture. No nothing.

"Only lucky if they have a pool. Come on." Kellog ran around to the back of the house. Birdie followed.

In the backyard, there was a kidney-shaped pool. Together they stood at the top and stared inside. "Different shape than the bowl at the skate park," Kellog observed.

"Gonna be interesting."

No one said anything for a minute.

"Does that mean you want to go first?" Kellog asked.

"I'm happy to go first, because I'm not a chicken."

"I'm just being polite. Ladies first."

Birdie rolled her eyes and pressed her left foot on the end of her board to make it stand vertical in the air.

"You gonna drop in? Dang, Nailsy. Starting off strong."

It was better not to overthink these things. Her motto: *Go. Just go.* She put her right foot on the top of the board and leaned her weight forward, zero hesitation, dropping herself into the pool.

"Woooo!" Kellog pumped his fist when she didn't fall.

They spent a while taking turns skating and getting the hang of the new shape. Eventually, Birdie tried to carve and grind on the tile at the top of the pool. But she kept sliding down before she made it, one time spinning out on her stomach. "Owww! Belly burn!!" she wailed. Finally, after what seemed like a million tries, she did it, the board making that satisfying scratch noise at the top.

"Heck, yeah! You are on fire, Nailsy!" Kellog shouted. "I wish I had a phone to record this stuff. That one was money. Get famous enough on YouTube, and companies will pay you to ride their boards and wear their clothes. Give you free stuff."

No one in their family even had a phone like that. Mama's wouldn't even text much less take photos or record video. And now that Mama was probably out of minutes, it might not even make calls.

After she accomplished what she'd set out to, she climbed out with her board and wandered around the backyard while Kellog continued to skate.

She got tired and sat down on a white iron bench and took out the sparkly-silver button from the tiny pocket in her army pants. They were her most comfortable pants for skating, though otherwise she hated them, because all the pockets were sewn shut. Faux pockets, her mother called them, for decoration only, which had to be the dumbest thing ever. Probably this was why someone had dropped them like a hot potato at the

Goodwill. But Birdie had been delighted to discover the pants did have one teeny, tiny pocket that opened—one exactly the right size for a sparkly-silver button.

Only it wasn't so sparkly anymore. She'd rubbed it so much the sparkles were almost gone. She'd even found some of the silver flecks ground so deep into her thumb that she'd had to scrub them out with soap. The tarnished button reminded her of the truth. She and Mama were in trouble. *Do you hear me, God? You have to help me and Mama. If you don't, we're going to be homeless.*

When she opened her eyes from praying, she spotted a cat. He was bright orange, and he waited by the back door of the house as if he was hoping to be let inside. She went to him and stroked his back. "Well, hello there, little guy." The cat swished against her legs, then leaned longingly against the door. And without thinking about it, Birdie tried the knob, and the door popped open. The cat scampered inside and up the stairs like he knew exactly where he was going.

"Oh no! Cat, come back!" She stepped through the doorway and paused. She'd done something stupid again. Because she couldn't shut the door and leave the cat closed up with no one to feed him.

The walls had holes like the one Birdie had made in Mrs. Hillmore's house, only the holes were everywhere. Water stains pooled on the ceiling in various places. There was a staircase with broken railings, like someone as impulsive as Birdie—but heavier—had used it as a slide. "Cat! Come, here!" Her voice echoed off the high ceilings. She climbed the stairs. It was strange, a house in Evercrest being in this horrible condition. What had happened to the family who'd lived there?

The carpets in the bedrooms were stained with rain or more likely pet urine from the smell. "Oh, Cat. Did you used to live here? Did your owners abandon you?" Maybe the cat had wandered off outside, while the owners packed up, and they couldn't find him before they'd moved away.

Poor thing. She had to help him. She wandered from empty room to empty room. Finally, she found him hugging against a particularly beat-up wall, more holes than she could count, torn plaster hanging like open wounds—as if someone with a sledge hammer had gotten mad or gone berserk. The cat leaned harder into the wall, meowing strangely. She crouched down to pet him, hoping he wouldn't bite her. But when she touched his bony ribs underneath his soft fur, he relaxed in her hands. "Shhhh, sweet kitty, it's okay. It's okay." She rubbed a hand along his back and up his tail, which had a crook in it. "Awe, you broke your tail? Poor kitty."

He stuck his nose into a small hole in the wall above the baseboard as if he intended to crawl inside to hide from his new cruel reality.

"It would be empty and lonely in there, too," she told

him. "Maybe you'd rather come home with me to get some food?"

The cat purred.

Now eye-level with the hole, Birdie saw something deep inside the wall. She sucked in a breath. Could it be?

Fortunately, the hole was just the right size for a small hand. Birdie plunged hers inside, clawing to the back of the wall. Eagerly, pushing and gripping, her fingers landing on a thick stack of papers. Unfortunately, too thick to be easily removed from the small hole. But rather than let go of what she'd found, Birdie punched backward with her hand.

Bam, punch.

Bam, punch.

Over and over, gripping the wad of paper tight, banging from the inside against the plaster until the wall gave way, and the paper could be freed. Her breath caught as she brought her treasure into the light.

And oh, what a treasure it was.

A fat stack of crisp hundred-dollar bills.

Birdie had never seen even one hundred-dollar bill in her life, much less a stack of them. Certainly not multiple stacks of them, because there was more inside the wall.

The light was dim, and she didn't trust her eyes, so she brought the stack she'd freed to the window.

It had started raining. Pouring cats and dogs actually, like it often did in Valley Lake, the sky just opening up, and soaking you to the bone in minutes. But despite the dark sky, she could see what was in her hand. It looked as real as the cat, who was swishing against her legs lest she forget he was hungry. The bills were wrapped in a yellow paper band. It slipped off easily, and hundred-dollar bills swirled in circles to the floor.

11

"Birdie!" Kellog called from downstairs.

Birdie jumped and thunder exploded outside the window.

Her hands reached for the bills that had fallen.

They pushed hurriedly at her pockets.

But all her pockets were sewn closed. All except the teeny, tiny one that held her silver button—a tiny pocket that might fit one of the bills if she had all day to spend folding it.

Which she didn't.

Of all the days to wear these dumb pants. Maybe God could have warned her that this would be the day she'd find a billion dollars hidden in a wall?

It had to go into her underwear.

She dropped in the stack then tucked and shoved the loose bills.

"What are you doing?" Kellog asked. He stood above her, dripping rain water onto the floor.

"Nothing." Birdie shot up straight, smashing her arms to her sides.

"You disappeared. I was hollering for you. Didn't you hear me?"

Birdie tugged at her shirt, trying to pull it over her lumpy butt. "No. Sorry, I was looking for this cat. I think he's been abandoned. I thought I'd take him home and feed him."

"Your mama is never going to let you keep him." Kellog leaned down to pet the cat behind his ears. But the cat must not have appreciated Kellog's wet hands, because he moved away.

"She might," Birdie insisted.

Kellog laughed. "I'm dying to be there when you ask her. You know this house has a lot of bedrooms. I swear I walked in half a dozen looking for you. I'm stuck sleeping on a sofa in our living room, when all these rich people have more rooms than they probably have people to sleep in them."

"Yeah." Birdie sympathized.

"A closet would be nice, at least," Kellog said.

Kellog's clothes hung on a rod right next to their sofa. It made their apartment look messy even when it was clean.

"And a door I could close," Kellog continued. "I can't sleep in. I can't talk on the phone without Mom hearing everything. I have to go to the bathroom to be alone, but since we only have one of those, it's not like I can be in there long."

Birdie nodded.

"What's wrong with you? You have a stomach ache or something?"

She had her arms crossed over her lower body, trying to keep her pants, heavy with money, from falling down. She wasn't in the habit of lying to Kellog, but if she told him about the money, he'd want half. And not that she was opposed to sharing, as a general rule, but God had sent this money to Mama. And Birdie wasn't sure how much Mama needed to never have to clean another house again. Kellog wouldn't understand. He'd want to spend it on skateboards and iPhones— who knew what else? So, she nodded. "Yeah, my stomach was just hurting for a second." She forced herself to let go of her pants hoping against hope none of the money would spill out.

"This house is crazy cool, isn't it?" Kellog asked.

"You mean a dump?"

"No, I mean cool." Kellog put his hand in one of the holes in the wall and ripped out a piece of plaster, making the hole even bigger than it was before.

"What are you doing?" Panic seized her heart.

"Helping them."

"Helping who?"

He put his hand in a different hole and ripped out another piece of wall. "Dad took me once to help him demolish a house. It was a blast."

Kellog's dad worked construction. Well, when he could find work. He always seemed to be *in between* jobs.

"Are you crazy? You can't destroy some random house for the fun of it." It was one thing to borrow someone's empty pool for skating. But it wasn't like Kellog to be a vandal.

"Trust me. I'm helping out. Someone like my dad is going to get *paid* to destroy this house. I mean look at it. How do you think all these holes got here anyway?"

"Someone got angry?" Birdie was trying to steer Kellog away from what she feared might be the truth—that someone had come looking for the money that she now hid in her underpants.

But Kellog took out one of those tiny pocket tools that flipped out knives and screwdrivers and proceeded to carve.

K. M. & B. L. were here

"Seriously, Kellog. Stop. I don't want my initials on the wall."

"No one's going to know it's us. And anyway, who-ever buys this house in *this* neighborhood will be filthy, stinking rich. They'll have the money to knock the whole place down and rebuild it all."

"Don't you want to go home to change your clothes? You're all wet."

"What? No, I'm fine. Dad says rich people always waste a bunch of money redoing everything, even when the place doesn't need it. And this house needs it."

It felt true. This rich neighborhood—every house with a pool, kids like Hailey who never had to worry about money—this incredible wealth was all around her. This world full of people so loaded they could buy a great big house and still have enough left over to redo everything just for the fun of it. She could see why Kellog was angry. She could see why he might want to carve up the wall. But she needed him to stop, so she said the only thing she could think of that might work.

"I think I have diarrhea."

12

"What?!" Kellog looked at Birdie like she'd just told him she wanted a cricket sandwich with a side of maggots. "That's disgusting!" And if Birdie hadn't been in such a desperate situation, she might have laughed.

"It's not *that* gross. I didn't go in my pants . . . yet. But I have to go home. There's no toilet paper in the bathrooms here."

Kellog straightened out his face and picked up his board. "Sure, of course." He glanced at the window. "It's stopped raining. Let's go."

Birdie picked up the cat with one arm, the other tugging down her shirt. "Can you carry my board for me?"

"What am I, your boyfriend? We're related, you know," Kellog said.

"Like I could forget. Now help out your blood relative by carrying something."

"Okay. You might need two hands to manage the cat." But after a few minutes, he said, "Huh. He's so calm. That's weird."

"What's weird?"

"That cat letting you hold him like that."

"Yeah?" Cats had always liked Birdie.

"They don't usually like to be picked up."

"He doesn't seem to mind."

"I see that."

Birdie smiled and snuggled her cat with the crooked tail a little closer.

"You're walking funny. Are you going to make it or are you going to poop your pants?" Kellog asked after they were a few houses down from the ruined gray house with the empty pool.

Birdie tried to walk faster toward the end of the street, toward Mrs. Hillmore's brilliant, green grass, the sun sparkling off the water-tipped blades.

But someone came speeding toward her on a skateboard. Jacob Powers? "Hey," she said, startled, but Jacob whizzed right by her.

"I can't stop. These jerks are chasing me!" he shouted.

Three white boys on heavily stickered skateboards

headed toward them. Birdie gripped her pants and clutched the cat to her chest. *Please God, let them skate on by.*

But God had done Birdie enough favors for today.

They stopped right in front of them.

"Hey, do you know that kid?" one of them in a Skate or Die T-shirt asked.

Birdie nodded. "He goes to my school."

Another, in cool black Vans shoes that Birdie wouldn't mind skating and dying in, added, "Then you must know he's a weeny."

The one in the Skate or Die shirt laughed. "Just like his brother Travis. Big weeny and little weeny."

"Are you two weenies, too?" the third one who had a chipped tooth and a strange way of talking asked. He peered at Birdie and Kellog like having a chipped tooth might not be all that was wrong with him. Like maybe for fun he tortured cats or younger kids until they spilled the location of hidden money.

She straightened her back, and tried to make her eyes look fierce. The worst thing she could do was look weak. "I think the only weeny here is you."

"Snap!" shouted Skate or Die.

The one with the chipped tooth took a step back. "Dang. Get a load of this girl."

"Ya'll just come from skating at the gray house?" Vans shoes wanted to know.

"You mean the house with the empty pool?" Kellog asked.

Birdie shot Kellog a surprised look, but he shrugged and mouthed, *What*? Like it was no big deal they'd been skateboarding in someone else's pool.

"These are the last days to enjoy it," the boy in the Vans said.

"What do you mean?" Birdie asked.

"House is going to be demolished on Tuesday."

Kellog shot Birdie a smug smile. "What'd I tell you? Why is it so messed up, do you know? How'd it get like that?"

"The old lady who lived in that house died." The one with the chipped tooth watched Birdie carefully, perhaps to see if this frightened her.

But old people died all the time.

"So, her sons moved in, but then the police came and hauled them off to jail in handcuffs. You should have seen it. There were cop cars all over the block. The whole house was surrounded."

"Wow!" Kellog said. "What did they do, rob a bank?"

The boy in the Skate or Die shirt ignored Kellog and slapped the one with the chipped tooth on the back. "Hush up, Dooker." Skate or Die leaned in to Birdie. "What's your name, little girl?"

"Birdie Loggerman." She jutted out her chest and tried hard not to look intimidated even though she was.

They were older than her and Kellog. Maybe thirteen or fourteen.

"We're not little. We're in seventh grade," Kellog said, which was a lie because they were both in sixth.

"Tell me your real grade, and we'll let you go."

Birdie frowned, because while she realized they were being held up, she hadn't realized they were being held hostage. "Let us go?"

"That's right. You can't pass until we know what grade you're in—for real."

"Sixth," Birdie said, because she didn't see why it mattered. She didn't need to be older to stand up for herself.

"Sixth grade! You hear that? These kids are begging for a bedtime story!"

"Yup, it's bedtime. Mama wanted us back," Birdie said. She didn't have all day to stand there and let these boys discover that the strange lumps protruding from her behind led to the only story worth telling.

"Ooooooh," the boys teased. "A mama's girl."

"Every girl has a mama and so does every boy. That's the circle of life."

"Ooooh, she told you!" Kellog said.

Dooker's creepy smile was replaced with a creepy frown.

Kellog, perhaps now appropriately fearing for their lives, finally got interested in hightailing it out of there. "Yeah, we gotta go. See you, fellas."

They hurried away as fast as Birdie's money-filled pants would allow.

Crossing a freeway with a meowing cat and piles of hundred-dollar bills shoved into her clothes was no easy feat. Especially when loose bills began to make their way down the legs of her pants and out the bottom.

Money swirled up behind her and flew across the road. Kellog was in front of her, so he didn't see. But behind her was a bus stop full of people. *Please don't let anyone notice.* Cars were coming, and she had to keep running.

13

On the other side of the highway, Birdie slowed down. She couldn't afford to lose any more of Mama's money and draw attention to herself. She hated that she hadn't been able to carry all of it. God had provided this amazing opportunity, and she was blowing it.

And Kellog was making Birdie sweat, being entirely too interested in those skater boys' story.

"What do you think those guys who got arrested did? A bunch of cops don't show up to drag you out of your own house like that unless you did something really bad."

Birdie nodded. "Maybe they escaped from jail." She

remembered the day Mama hadn't let her play outside in Mrs. Hillmore's neighborhood. There wasn't a lot of crime in Valley Lake, particularly not in Evercrest. It had to be connected.

"That's stupid. You should know better than anyone once you go to jail, they throw away the key."

Kellog was talking about Birdie's father. Rick was locked up at Polkville Men's Correctional Institute where he'd probably stay for the rest of his life because that's what happened when you held up a convenience store with a gun and shot the cashier in the shoulder.

Rather than argue with Kellog, it seemed better to nod and hope he lost interest.

"And anyway, if they escaped, why would they go home? That would be the first place the cops would look."

Normally, true. But what if they had to retrieve a bunch of hidden money first? A realization dawned on Birdie. Of course.

The money she'd found was stolen.

She hadn't known that God acted like Robin Hood, taking money from criminals and giving it to the poor. Well, okay, that wasn't exactly right. Robin Hood had stolen it from the rich and given it to the poor, but God had an even smarter idea. Criminals didn't deserve it, and she and Mama did.

But after a while Birdie got to wondering what

Mama would say about all this when she found out. And then she got to wondering what to tell Mama and what not to tell Mama. She hated to leave things out or, heaven forbid, outright lie to Mama. But if Mama found out this money was from evil-doing criminals, she might not want it. Dirty money, she'd call it, like the kind she'd refused to take from no-good Rick. Mama had been worried enough lately. Birdie didn't want her to worry anymore.

When they got back to Woodcroft, Birdie tore into the house without saying hi to Mama or Aunt Laura. She raced for the bathroom, leaving Kellog to stand in the doorway holding the stray cat.

She slammed the bathroom door and dumped all the money she'd found out of her pants. She stuffed it into the bathroom cabinets way at the back behind the extra rolls of toilet paper. She didn't have time to count it or lay it neat; she just needed it out of her pants and out of sight. Then she flushed the toilet. Twice.

"Do you want some Pepto-Bismol?" Mama asked when she came out.

Birdie shook her head.

"You sure? You look a little green." Aunt Laura dug into her purse. "I've got some mint gum in here some-where, always settles my stomach."

"No, thanks." Birdie wished she could stuff her hands in some pockets. But she was still wearing the dumbest pants on the planet. Instead she tucked her thumbs into her belt loops. "Maybe you guys should head home before it gets dark? It's a pretty long drive."

"Birdie!" Mama said. "What's gotten into you? They've come all this way to see us. We aren't going to send them home without dinner. And it's not like you to bring home stray animals. You know we can't afford to keep a cat."

"He's starving, Mama," Birdie whined. "He can have my dinner. I won't eat. Can I please go lie down?"

"I told you she fell hard for this guy," Kellog said, stroking the cat's head.

Mama looked at Birdie like she wasn't acting like herself, which she wasn't.

"Thank you for coming to visit, Aunt Laura and Kellog."

"Anytime, honey. Feel better, okay?"

She gave them both a hug, and Kellog whispered in her ear that he would keep trying to convince Mama about the cat. Then she went as fast as she could to her room, closed the door, and let out a breath so deep it felt like she'd been holding it her whole life.

14

At some point after dinner, Mama knocked on Birdie's door. Birdie pretended to be asleep because she was afraid Mama might ask questions that she would have to lie to answer.

The door opened, and she felt something four-legged pounce onto the bed.

Next a soft kiss from Mama. "Only for tonight," Mama whispered.

Inside, Birdie smiled. Tonight was all she needed. Tomorrow they'd have enough money to feed a dozen cats.

The cat purred against her as she rubbed him. "You hear that, Cat? Tomorrow we're rich."

Her bookbag lay by the dresser, empty and waiting.

"Tomorrow I'll buy you your own bed to snuggle in while Mama and I watch *Downton Abbey* and *Let's Go Home* on TV. And I'll buy you nice food and treats. So many treats. What flavor would you like?"

The cat yowled like he was trying to answer.

Birdie cocked her head. "Well, okay. If you insist, I'll buy you one of everything."

He meowed again.

"Yes, yes. Don't worry, we can afford it. No problem." She laughed and rubbed her face in the cat's fur.

He cuddled into her.

She lay with him quietly, enjoying the synchronized sound of their breathing.

When all was silent, she slipped out of her room, her bookbag in hand. She retrieved the money from the bathroom. She counted the stack along with the loose bills. But maybe she'd counted wrong. She counted again. Twenty thousand dollars?

It was unbelievable.

Such an incredible amount of money. And so much more was hidden in that wall.

Lying in bed again, pajamas on, covers drawn tight, she tried to relax. Breathe. In and out. In and out.

Tomorrow she'd get the rest. She closed her eyes. Tomorrow everything would change. Tomorrow she and Mama would be rich.

At first light, in her hazy, mind-jumbled state, it was easy for it all to seem not quite real. Maybe there was no money. Maybe she couldn't trust herself.

She stared at the still-sleeping cat as if he weren't real either and might poof into thin air if she looked away. *Shhhhh,* she said with her finger to her lips like he might wake up meowing. She crept over to her bookbag and unzipped it. At the sight of all those crisp bills, her heart picked up speed and threatened to skate out of her chest.

She closed her eyes and opened them again.

She held a stack of hundreds in her hand. Solid. Real.

The cat jumped off the bed and wandered over. He tried to hop in the bag.

"Come out of there. You can't give me away," she whispered.

He backed up slowly, stretching out long. Then he followed her to the bathroom where she took a shower and got ready for school.

She said hello to Mama and choked down the last of the cereal from their nearly empty pantry.

"How's your stomach today?"

"Good."

Mama looked at her meaningfully. "If you want to stay home, you can. I can't imagine anything worse than having diarrhea at school."

"I'm fine."

"Okay, if you're sure. Hey, what did you end up doing with those business cards you took from my purse?" Mama asked.

Birdie paused. She hadn't realized Mama knew she took them. Was Mama saying that it was okay to steal things if you had a really good reason? "I gave them to some of my friends who are rich enough to afford a cleaner."

"Did anything come of it?"

"No." She'd checked and double-checked with everyone except Hailey. There was no point checking with Hailey. "They all already have someone to clean their houses."

Mama chewed her lip.

"What's wrong? Don't you think someone will call soon?" She wished she could tell Mama right now that she didn't need to worry anymore.

"I'm sure they will. Clean as a Whistle won't give me a good reference, but somehow, it'll work out. Someone will see that I'm trustworthy."

"You *are* trustworthy, Mama. You didn't try to hide what I'd done at Mrs. Hillmore's house. You called her right away."

Mama nodded. "And I don't regret it. I've got my integrity if nothing else." After a few minutes, she said, "Your cat was so quiet last night. I was thinking how glad I am you didn't bring home a barky dog."

Birdie smiled. She'd found a can of tuna in the back of the pantry, which the cat was currently gobbling up. She had to figure out a way to get this money to Mama so they could buy him some actual cat food—and all those treats she'd promised him.

"Oh, I almost forgot. I gave Jessie's phone number to Aunt Laura so they can reach us. He said Kellog called you last night after he and Aunt Laura drove back to Polkville, but you were already in bed. Do you want to go over to Jessie's to call him back? You could probably catch Kellog before school."

"No. I gotta go." She didn't want to call Kellog. It was easier to keep things from him if she didn't talk to him.

When she picked up her board, the cat meowed. Birdie leaned down to rub his ears, his back, and his crooked tail. "I'd take you, but they don't allow cats in school. I'm sorry. You'll have to stay here with Mama."

"Come here. I'll take good care of you." Mama patted her lap but seemed shocked when the cat actually obeyed and leapt up. She rubbed his back. "He's so friendly. I've never seen anything like it."

"I know. He's great. I can keep him, right?"

Mama rolled her eyes and smiled. "We'll see."

On her way out, Birdie noticed a letter on the table by the door. "Do you want me to mail this for you?" she called back to Mama in the kitchen.

"No, I'll do it!"

Birdie saw that the envelope had a handwritten address on flowered stationery. She hadn't known that Mama owned stationery, because as far as she knew, Mama didn't write letters. She was highly curious as to who Mama would be writing to, but instead of peeking at the letter again like she normally might, she looked away. Mama had her secrets.

And Birdie had hers.

15

On her way to the bus stop, she passed the Woodcroft tenant mailboxes. They were down on the street so the mailman could toss each unit's mail in quickly and speed out of there as fast as he could drive. The boxes were always getting broken into because they were in a lonely spot, and the backside opened up with a simple twist of a crowbar. The backside was open now. Junk mail littered the ground, and all the boxes looked rifled through. Mama always joked that all they ever got in the mail were bills, and she sure hoped the thief would pay one or two of them for her.

"Hey, Little Bird."

"Hey, Jessie."

He had his mail key in his hand, and he was dressed in his security guard uniform like he was about to go to work. "Looks like our mail got tampered with again. They better not have taken my winning sweepstakes letter."

Birdie laughed. "Hope they didn't take mine either." And with that thought, a new more useful one appeared.

What if she mailed Mama the money? Not in a letter, easy to steal, but in a package—maybe the kind that got delivered straight to your door. If she put it in a thick box, no one would know it was cash.

That way Mama could put the money into her own bank account.

Jessie leaned down to pick up some of the scattered mail, checking who it was addressed to and putting it back in the proper box.

"Why do you like helping people so much anyway?"

"I guess I think whoever dies with the most friends wins."

"Wins what?"

Jessie chuckled. "I don't know. I'm not dead yet."

"Do you help people at your job?" Birdie asked. Jessie worked at the Valley Lake mall—the one with all the ritzy stores. It was one of the reasons Mama trusted him so much. He had to go through an extensive background check in order to work security there.

"Not really," Jessie said slowly like he'd rather he had a job where he could be more helpful.

The ritzy mall was so safe, being a security guard there was probably pretty boring. "You ever wish someone would up and rob the jewelry store? Make off with a load of diamonds so you'd have to tackle them to save the day?"

Jessie's face lit up. "Yeah! I could use some excitement like that, you know?"

"I could rob it for you," Birdie joked. "Only it would be better if you didn't tackle me."

Jessie laughed. "You wouldn't do something like that, Little Bird."

But Birdie wasn't sure. If she hadn't found this money for Mama, maybe she would have.

She waved 'bye to Jessie and found the school bus waiting for her when she arrived at the stop. But instead of hopping on, she tossed her board to the ground and took off in the opposite direction.

"Hey, bag lady, where you going?" someone yelled from the bus window. "School is this way!"

It sounded like Aiden Fuller, but Birdie didn't turn around to find out. She wasn't going to answer to bag lady. As soon as she got the money to Mama, she could throw a great big party and invite the whole class. There'd be catered food just like there'd be at Hailey's parents' annual Winter Wonderland party. Then Aiden would know that he should be nice to her if he wanted to be invited back.

The highway was busy with cars, but Birdie skated onward. *Go fast,* she told herself. *Go so, super-duper-freaking fast.*

She pushed her foot against the road over and over until she had a good speed going. Her right foot (instinct) guided her as her left foot (adrenaline) followed along. Until her hair flew out behind her like a cape. She was a brave girl on a brave mission.

And before long, her apartment at Woodcroft was behind her, and the gray house in Evercrest was in front of her.

She jumped off her board, and tip-toe-ran to the back of the house. Even though she'd stopped skating, the rush of the wind whipping all around her remained. And the feeling of the wheels turning and rushing stayed in her bones as she ran up the stairs.

Breathless, she reached the room with the hidden money. She crouched low.

Every bill was still there.

Those mean neighborhood boys hadn't found it.

She reached her hand in the wall, took the money out, and filled her bag to bursting. She didn't take time to count it. She only took time to zip her bag and run for the door. But then she remembered her initials on the wall.

She hadn't brought a knife or anything to scratch over it with. Maybe she could find a sharp rock outside in the yard. Down the stairs and out the back door, she stared out over the pool. Concrete, nothing but concrete.

A car engine. It sounded close, too close. She walked to the front yard.

A car door slammed. Her eyes landed on the back of a man, his dark jacket showing a white science symbol that she thought might represent a nuclear atom. He spun around. "Hey, you!" he yelled.

She shot off like a bullet, racing through the tangled yard. Her wheels finally under her as she hit the wide street with her board. Her leg pushed out once, twice, fighting to gain speed.

Birdie's foot shot out again to peddle the board, the wheels speeding up beneath her. Her right foot aiming, her left foot following. Out, out, out.

"Kid!" He ran forward a few steps. "I know you can hear me! Hey! Come back! I need to talk to you."

Push. Ride. Push. Ride. Push.

"I just want to talk to you!"

Ride. Push. Ride. Push. Ride.

Stop. Look both ways.

She raced across the highway, carrying her board.

Safely on the other side, she jumped back on, wheels turning again, her hair flying. Every time a car passed, she panic prayed. *Please don't be him. Please don't be him.*

16

Thump. Thump. Thump. Thump. It took a little while for her heart to slow, for adrenaline to stop driving. For instinct to take a back seat, too.

But finally, she didn't think she was being followed, and she arrived at the shopping center where there was a Ship It store next to the laundromat. She took comfort in the normal bustle of customers coming in and out of places. Her initials were still on that wall, but there was nothing she could do about it now. She wouldn't go back to that house. Ever.

She popped her skateboard up into her hand, coming to a stop at the store's entrance. She'd spent many hours looking in the windows of the Ship It, waiting for her and Mama's laundry to finish next door. It wasn't that exciting looking at cardboard boxes of varying sizes and prices, but now she was glad that she had paid attention.

She approached the counter, slowed her breathing, and made her voice calm. "I'd like to ship something, please."

There was a thin white man behind the counter with his back to her. But when he turned around, her breath caught. He wasn't a man. He was Jacob's brother, Travis. What was he doing there? He seemed too young to be running a cash register.

"What do you want?" Travis's face darkened under his dark hair, as if he didn't like seeing Birdie any better than she liked seeing him.

She wanted to leave. Maybe hide in a cave somewhere. But this was the only shipping place she knew of, and she needed to get Mama this money before something happened to it. "I need to ship something." Her voice was a battle cry. She would not back down. She would not be scared away.

Travis groaned and slid her a form and a pen.

"Shouldn't you be in school?" Birdie asked him, which was a bold question considering where she herself should be.

"I don't go to school," he replied, not looking up from some papers he seemed to be pretending to straighten.

"Oh," Birdie said, though it didn't seem like it could be true.

Travis eyed the empty form. "You gonna fill that out or what?"

"Actually, I hurt my hand skateboarding. Could you fill it out for me?" She couldn't risk Mama recognizing her handwriting.

"Oh, come on. Really?" Travis pushed his hair from his face and sighed deeply. But he took the form and wrote in what Birdie told him. But when he asked her what return address to use, Birdie clammed up.

"You gotta have a name and return address," he insisted.

"What if I'm sending something to myself?" Birdie asked.

Travis stared at her a long beat. "Like a time capsule? We can't hold your package for ten years. Longest we can wait to ship is a day."

"Ten years?!" Birdie shook her head because she didn't know what Jacob's crazy brother was talking about. "I need it to arrive today."

"Soonest it can arrive is tomorrow evening." Travis looked at the form again. "This address isn't that far from here. You could put that skateboard of yours to use and drop it off yourself."

"No, I can't do that!" Birdie said too loud.

He held up his hands like Birdie was robbing him. "Okay, geez, it was just an idea. Next-day shipping is going to cost you serious bucks is all."

"Everything okay out there?" A male voice came from a closed-off area behind the counter.

"Yeah, everything's fine, Dad," Travis shouted back.

"If you're not nice to the customers, I'm closing the shop and driving you straight to school!"

Birdie couldn't help smiling that Travis had been caught in his lie. "I got money," she said.

"You still have to put a sender's name and address, and it has to be different than the *ship to* address in case we have a problem with delivery."

Birdie paused, watching as he hovered the pen over the form. "Are you sure?" She half hoped the voice would come from the back again, demanding that Travis do as she asked.

"Of course, I'm sure. Maybe you can use your grandmother's address?"

"My grandmother's dead."

"Your grandfather?" he asked.

"He's in an old folks' home in Ohio, so we never visit. I don't know the address."

"You're a real sob story, aren't you?"

"You're supposed to be nice to me, remember?" Birdie said.

Travis rolled his eyes. "You want to use the Ship It store address? If the package gets sent back here, I can call you."

"Oh! That's a good idea. See, you can be helpful if you want to be."

"What size box?"

"Medium?" Birdie had already decided she wasn't going to ship all the money in the same package. She'd ship one, make sure it arrived, and then she'd ship another, then another.

"Do you have a restroom?" Birdie asked.

"Sorry. Closest one is next door at the laundromat."

"I'll be right back," Birdie said.

"Hey! You have to pay for that box first."

Birdie stayed by the door so he couldn't see as she knelt to open her backpack and carefully slid a hundred-dollar bill from underneath the yellow wrapped paper. She walked back to the counter, willing her knees not to give way, the bill stiff as starched cotton in her hand.

"Wow, poor girl is rolling with the big bucks," Travis marveled, taking the cash and holding it up to the light to check for who knew what exactly.

The thought that the money might be counterfeit made Birdie weak at the knees again, and the room appeared to spin. She grabbed the counter.

"Can't be too careful," Travis said finally, lowering the money.

Relief shot through Birdie like a drug.

He typed something into the cash register, and it popped open to give Birdie her change.

And what a pile of change it was.

Birdie was wearing her dumb pants without pockets again, so she had to chuck the money in the cardboard box rather than open up her backpack. Despite wanting to prove even further to Jacob's mean brother that Birdie Loggerman wasn't anything close to a poor girl anymore, she couldn't risk it. She needed Mama to have every cent safely tucked into her bank account first. Then she'd show Travis Powers and everyone else in Valley Lake a thing or two.

At the laundromat, Birdie made a beeline for the restroom, where perched on top of a closed toilet seat, she discovered just how rich she and Mama might be. Once, twice, three times, she counted a fresh stack of the hundreds. Each time she got a hundred hundreds.

All the stacks appeared the same size about half an inch thick. There were fifty stacks in the bottom of her bag. Math like this was easy. It was the kind where all you had to do was keep adding zeros . . . and zeros . . . and zeros. Until the number was so big that Birdie nearly fell off the toilet seat in shock. Could it be? Was she really carrying around half a million dollars?

Birdie felt a stab of guilt that she hadn't shared some of
the money with Kellog. He and Aunt Laura needed it
nearly as bad as her and Mama. Well, she could always
suggest to Mama they share once Mama's bank account
was full.

With her hand open as wide as she could get it, she
could hold eight stacks, eighty thousand dollars, all in
one hand. It was crazy to hold so much money at once,
but strangely, it didn't look like much. And it really
didn't look like much thrown to the bottom of a cardboard box. Still, it was a ton of money to lose if it went
missing in the mail or got stolen. Decision time. How
much should she send to Mama?

Five shipments of ten stacks, one hundred thousand dollars each, seemed right. But it only filled about a third of the box. If Birdie were playing one of those games where you had to guess how many jelly beans were in the jar, she would've failed miserably at guessing there was one hundred thousand dollars in the box. But as lonely as it looked, it was as much as she could bring herself to ship at a time.

It just needed company was all. Something to keep it from rattling around in there and sounding so much like money. Something to hide it if someone looked inside. She hopped off the toilet and opened the stall door to look for some paper towels. But the bathroom only had a hand blow dryer. Okay. She'd have to get resourceful.

In the laundromat she surveyed the customers. Mama would kill her for talking to a stranger by herself like this, but she would be smart. She would pick someone who looked harmless. She spotted an older lady in thick glasses who seemed like she might be the type to bake her own donuts. Donut lady was pulling her clothes out of the dryer.

"I'll give you a hundred dollars for some of your shirts." Birdie didn't want the lady to say no. She held the cardboard box close so the lid would stay down, her skateboard under her arm, the money extended.

"What? Why?" the lady asked. "They won't fit you, honey."

"I just need a few for padding," Birdie said. "I'm mailing something breakable."

"Oh, well, okay," the lady said. She eyed the hundred-dollar bill. "You can have some of my husband's clothes. But they aren't worth all that, and I don't have change."

"It's yours." Birdie couldn't reveal her stash. She snatched up some clothes and ran back to the restroom to hide the stacks of money inside shirtsleeves and pants legs. This way if Travis or anyone else got curious and opened her box, they wouldn't think it was anything special.

"You again," Travis said when she returned like she was back just to annoy him.

But Birdie's good mood couldn't be rocked. Mama's first box of money was ready to go. And she couldn't wait to see Mama's face when she opened it.

18

Birdie was about to skate off to school when she remembered that she couldn't just show up two hours late. She needed a note. As much as she hated to go back into the Ship It store, Travis might be her only hope. Donut lady didn't look like the type to agree to forgery.

She pushed open the door. *Go. Just go.* "Can you sign a sick note for me?" Her voice was low so Mr. Powers couldn't hear from the back.

Travis smirked like he'd been waiting his whole life for someone to ask him something he could laugh and say no to. But to her surprise he grabbed a pen and said, "What do you want to be sick with?"

In the end they decided she'd been to the dentist.

Birdie dashed out of there with the note and hopped on her board. She'd never skateboarded so fast. Not because she was late to school, but because the feeling of someone following her, someone chasing her, wouldn't let up. She craned her neck to look behind her so often that she had a near miss with a no-parking sign. She didn't know how she didn't ride right through it. After that she tried to keep her eyes forward, but it was hard. What if that guy was still after her?

At Valley Lake Elementary, Mrs. Alverez greeted her in the front office. It was all Birdie could do not to visibly shake. "I've been careful to think before I speak like we talked about," Birdie said, hoping to distract the assistant principal from reading her note too closely.

Mrs. Alverez smiled. "I'm glad to hear that." And she sent Birdie off to class with the all clear, just like that, no hesitation.

A hundred-thousand dollars mailed off to Mama, and four hundred thousand still on her back, she'd gotten away with it. And with her safe inside the school hidden from the man in the nuclear atom jacket, everything was right with the world. That was until the lunch lady noticed her bookbag. "Sorry, no backpacks in the cafeteria."

"Please," Birdie begged. "I was absent this morning, and I have to catch up on some work." Panic rose in her chest. The last thing she needed was to be parted from so much money. It wasn't like her cubby had a lock. Someone could go through her bag. It could be stolen, or she could get into God knows how much trouble.

But by some miracle Mrs. Alverez appeared and nodded to the lunch lady. "It's okay. Let her have it."

"Thank you," Birdie said. "Thank you so much." And she raced to the lunch line before Mrs. Alverez or the lunch lady developed X-ray vision.

Everyone seemed to be staring at her all the time— that was the thing about carrying around such an enormous pile of money.

And Jacob was the worst offender. He stopped by the girls' table at lunch, even being so bold as to set his tray in the empty space across from hers.

"Missed you this morning," he said with a fox's smile like Travis had texted him that she'd been skipping.

While it was nice to have something else to focus on so it wouldn't look like she was listening to Hailey's steal-the-show conversation at the other end of the table, Jacob Powers wasn't exactly her first choice for a distraction.

Apparently, Hailey's parents' annual Winter Wonderland party was on Saturday afternoon. Birdie didn't have to ask to know that she wasn't invited, which was literally the worst. She hadn't gotten to go last year because she didn't live in Valley Lake then. And from the way everyone talked about it, it sounded like the most amazing party of all time.

But as soon as Jacob showed up, the girls stopped talking, and now they were all listening to Birdie's conversation.

"Go away," Birdie said.

"I wrote down the homework assignment for you that we got in first period." Jacob produced a folded piece of paper from his pocket and tossed it on her tray.

Birdie eyed it like it was a bottle rocket. After a few seconds in which it did not blast off into her face, she looked up to say thank you, but Jacob had already walked away.

"That was super nice," Lily said, breaking the girls' silence, not even trying to pretend like she hadn't been listening.

Apparently, eavesdropping wasn't a sin.

Maybe this was Jacob's way of saying sorry. Although he owed Hailey a bigger apology than he did Birdie. She snuck a glance at Hailey. Birdie also owed Hailey an apology. But since Hailey's mother wouldn't allow them to talk, she couldn't figure out how. There was never a chance when no one else was around.

It was probably pointless anyway. Hailey wouldn't even meet her gaze. It looked like Hailey's mom had bought her brand-new fuzzy boots, since her others had been ruined in the lake. And Hailey stared down at them under the table as if they were the most fascinating things on earth.

Birdie wondered what Mrs. Kirkland would say if

she found out Birdie was rich now. Would she allow her to be friends with Hailey again? Birdie wanted to try one of the cranberry-orange scones at Hailey's Winter Wonderland party or a chocolate-dipped marshmallow with snowflake sprinkles. Maybe Birdie should've mailed all the money to Mama in one big pile.

Birdie wanted to be rich enough by Saturday.

The bus arrived at Woodcroft, and Birdie raced through the littered parking lot, over the unmowed grass, and up the stairs to her and Mama's apartment. Her heart hammering, the money smacking her back, her skateboard tight under her arm, she'd run so freaking fast in case the man from the gray house had figured out where she lived. Kellog had drawn their initials. The guy could have asked around about her. Those neighborhood kids knew she'd been to the abandoned house. They knew her name and what school she attended. The man in the nuclear atom jacket could be watching her right now, just waiting to pounce.

She swung the door open, startling the cat who looked like he might actually pounce. *Oh, Cat.* It felt so good to bury her nose in his fur. She wanted to hide there forever, safe and snug, but Mama said Kellog had called again. "I have too much homework to talk on the phone," she lied while staring at her feet, which caused Mama to also look at Birdie's feet.

"Wow. Those sneakers have really had it. The rubber's peeling off the side on that one." Mama pointed to Birdie's right foot. "Don't you have other shoes?"

"No. You were going to take me shopping when you got paid. Remember?" Birdie said, then quickly added, "But I don't mind waiting. They're okay."

"They're really not. I better take you."

"We can't afford it," Birdie said as she headed to her room with her bookbag before Mama could notice it was heavier than usual.

Mama followed her. "You let me decide what we can and can't afford, okay?" The cat also followed her and bounded onto the bed like he couldn't wait for them to snuggle there. "Pretty soon your foot's going to fall right out with that rubber peeling like that."

Birdie shrugged. "I can duct-tape them if I have to."

Mama looked Birdie up and down like she'd gotten taller overnight. "Well, that's a resourceful idea. But don't you *want* new sneakers?"

"I understand we need more important things . . . like food and gas . . . and cat food."

"Speaking of that, I bought some and a litter box, and I got you cereal."

Birdie gave Mama a hug. "Cereal and cat food are all I need." And they really needed that litter box. She hadn't wanted to tell Mama, but the cat had pooped in the potted plant.

When Birdie pulled away, there were tears in Mama's eyes.

It broke Birdie's heart. Mama thought she was some big hero, but like everything lately, it was a lie. Would God like it that she was lying so much? Maybe He didn't mind if she was lying to protect someone. Similar to how if she prayed for someone else that was okay. It had to be. How else would she get Mama the money without worrying her?

In this case, though, she'd lied about not wanting new shoes. And she'd done it because she'd rather wait on the cash that was going to arrive on their doorstep tomorrow so she could buy the best skater shoes in the store *and* fuzzy boots like Hailey's. If she let Mama take her shoe shopping now, she would end up with the bargain-basement special from Foot Mart. And shoes like that would not get her invited over to the Kirklands' house. She'd lied this time to protect herself.

It wasn't right. She opened her mouth to undo it.

She had to undo it.

But instead she looked down at her dusty, old shoes and imagined what it would be like to be looking at brand-new shoes that she actually wanted. She'd never had shoes she actually wanted. She pressed her lips together. She said nothing. She left one more lie out there to simmer over the fire.

19

The next day, Birdie rushed home from school, as fast as she could run, checking over her shoulder like always. Travis had said the package would arrive by seven p.m., but what if Mama was out interviewing for a job and had already missed the delivery? Ugh, Birdie should have come up with some reason why Mama had to stay home.

She ran up the stairs and opened the door to find Mama vacuuming the carpet in another of her wildly colored dresses. This one looked like summer with bright yellow suns and fluorescent green grass. The vacuum was so loud Mama didn't even look up when Birdie entered.

"Mama, you can't even hear the door with that thing on."

"I'm sorry, sweetie. The floor was dirty."

"What if someone tried to knock?"

"Then I hope they went away," Mama said.

"Mama!" Birdie had forgotten that they were avoiding rent collectors.

Mama looked surprised like she hadn't meant to let on so much. "Everything's going to be fine, sweetheart. I got a few job leads today. They'll pan out soon enough. Is there another notice envelope on the door?"

Birdie paused. Another notice envelope? She didn't know there'd been a first one. "No, I just—I asked Jessie to come over if he found any of our mail on the ground. The boxes got broken into again." The lies were coming out smooth as the worn rubber on the bottom of her sneakers. She could see that Mama believed her. It gave her a weird feeling, like this dream she had once where she went skateboarding in the clouds. But her board kept wrecking them until there weren't any clouds left, and she woke up falling.

"Well, that would be nice if Jessie came over." Mama unplugged the vacuum and began to wrap up the cord.

The cat came out from under the couch where he'd been hiding from the vacuum. Birdie rushed over to pet him, and after that all was quiet.

Dinner that night was quiet, too. They ate rice and these spotted beans that had been in the back of the pantry for ages. Birdie didn't even know why they had them. They looked weird, but weren't bad. And for dessert they had applesauce, which wasn't normal, but whatever; soon they could have a bakery cake every night if they wanted.

After dinner Mama turned on the TV to watch *Downton Abbey*. She even kept the volume down lower than usual, which Birdie appreciated more than she could say.

Finally, when Birdie thought she might scream if something didn't happen soon, there was a loud *thunk*.

Birdie flew up off the couch and flung open the door. Her box for Mama had been dropped or more probably thrown, as the driver was already gone.

"It's addressed to you," Birdie said.

"That's strange. I didn't order anything." Mama joined Birdie at the door.

It was all Birdie could do not to jump up and down shouting, *we're rich, we're rich!* or at the very least to breathe down Mama's neck as she sat at the kitchen table and tore into the box. But she forced herself to open the pantry and pretend to dig for a snack.

From the corner of her eye she could see Mama had pulled out some of the clothes that Birdie had stuffed in the box. She held up a pair of boxer shorts with a bear

117

pumping gas into a pickup truck. The words *Gas Station* were printed across the butt, and an expression of utter confusion planted itself on Mama's face.

"Huh," Mama said as she stared at a pair of pajama bottoms covered in chickens. The top of the box had filler clothes. Birdie had stuffed the shirts and pants with the stacks of money in the bottom. It took so much willpower not to jump in and explain, because with each new piece of clothing, Mama's expression of confusion deepened.

Mama checked the return label. "All it says is the address of a Ship It store. What guy would mail me his clothes? How strange." Mama stood up. "I'm going to talk to Jessie—maybe he knows something about this. You stay here."

Birdie's mouth opened, then shut again. What were the words she could say? It hadn't occurred to her that Mama might not find the money—that she'd tucked it all too tightly in the sleeves and pants legs at the bottom of the box, and Mama wouldn't take the time to figure out that the real gift wasn't chicken pajamas.

But Mama was gone before she'd even taken all the clothes from the box.

Birdie tried to imagine the conversation Mama might be having with Jessie right now. She didn't know whether she should laugh or cry.

Until she realized this was her chance. A golden opportunity to make them even richer. She dashed to her room and grabbed some more stacks of money and buried them under the remaining clothes.

In moments, Mama was back. "What are you doing?"

"Sorry, I didn't mean to be nosey, but there's something you gotta see here."

Mama reached her hand into the box just like Birdie had reached into the wall, pulling out dreamland amounts of cash. "Oh my god," Mama breathed, the words soft-cloud whispers of disbelief. "I had no idea he'd really come through for us in such a big way."

"Who?" Birdie asked.

Mama dumped out the rest of the box, then looked up at Birdie like she'd forgotten she was there.

"I'm in shock."

"Me, too," Birdie agreed. "What did Jessie say?"

"He wasn't home, so I called him at work. I used the last two minutes on my phone to find out that he doesn't know anything about a box full of clothes. I ignored Aunt Laura's call the other day to save minutes for an emergency. Now we can't call anyone if the car breaks down."

Their car broke down a lot, so Mama had been smart to save minutes. But now they could buy a brand-new car if they wanted to. Mama just didn't know it yet. "It'll be okay, Mama. I promise. It really will. You believe Jessie. Don't you?"

Mama stared down at the sizable pile of cash on their kitchen table. "I do now."

"Then who do you think sent it?"

"I can't know for sure, but—"

"I can," Birdie said.

Mama tipped her head toward Birdie in confusion.

"God," Birdie announced. "I prayed for money just like Lily said I should—"

"Lily told you to pray for money?"

"Well, yeah, kind of. She said if I prayed for someone else, my prayer would be answered. So, I prayed for money . . . for you, not for me. And look—" Birdie spread out her arms, "—it worked."

"Well, I have a different theory."

"You do?"

"Yes. I wrote to your grandfather. He must have sent us this money. Though I've never known him to have a sense of humor—" Mama held up the boxer shorts with the words *Gas Station* printed across the butt, "—but maybe he's gotten funny in his old age . . . or he just farts more."

They both laughed.

But then Mama got serious. "It's awful that I hardly know him anymore, and we never get to see him."

"Yeah," Birdie agreed. Now that he was in an old folks' home and didn't have a place for them to stay, affording a hotel plus gas all the way to Ohio were more than Mama could manage. Birdie motioned to the cash. "But now we have the money to visit!"

"We sure do."

Birdie wondered what would happen when Mama called and found out that Grandpa didn't know anything about gas-station boxer shorts, some chicken pajamas, and a huge pile of hundred-dollar bills.

20

Birdie had the hundreds laid out neatly in ten stacks of ten. Or at least they used to be neat before the cat jumped on the table and knocked them around. He pawed at them playfully with his cute orange-and-white feet. "Grand total?"

"A hundred fifty thousand," Mama said. In her hand was the same calculator she'd used only weeks ago to add up their monthly expenses—probably realizing that they couldn't afford a basic thing like trash pickup.

Birdie whooped. Finally, they were rich, and she could shout about it. "We can throw a party!"

"Now, wait a minute." Mama looked serious. "We can't be careless until I get a job. And we don't know how long that will take. It's a lot of money, but if I'm out of work for months and months, it could go fast."

"But, Mama," Birdie said, extremely disappointed. She didn't want to be careless, but she wanted Mrs. Kirkland to understand that she wasn't poor anymore so she and Hailey could be friends again. She wanted to be invited to the Kirklands' Winter Wonderland party. And the only way that was going to happen was if she proved she was worthy to Mrs. Kirkland. "I want to buy Hailey a really nice present."

"Is it her birthday?"

"No."

"Birdie, really," Mama said, clearly exasperated. "You aren't listening. We start throwing money into the air, buying presents for people for no reason, this money will be gone so fast we'll hardly know we had it. It's like those people who win the Powerball or Mega Millions and are penniless in a year."

Birdie folded her arms over her chest and frowned. "Well, what's the point of having money if we aren't going to spend it?" She didn't want to be poor anymore. And anyway, soon she'd be sending Mama more boxes with stacks of money, so Mama didn't need to worry.

But it *was* Mama's money after all, and maybe it wasn't right for Birdie to take even a penny of it for herself. But Birdie *really* wanted to make things right with Hailey.

"Why do you want to buy her a present?" Mama asked.

Birdie lowered her head. "I lost all my friends when I said the bad word at school. I thought maybe if I bought Hailey something really nice, she'd forgive me."

"Oh, sweetheart." Mama pulled Birdie in close, and Birdie burst into tears.

"Hailey hates me," Birdie cried.

"Everything's going to be okay," Mama whispered, patting Birdie's back to comfort her. "You can get Hailey a little something and yourself some school clothes. I'd planned to take you shopping before all this happened." Mama slid a hundred-dollar bill from one of the stacks and handed it to Birdie.

Birdie knew how to bargain shop so that twenty dollars spent like a hundred. With a hundred dollars, she could buy the moon.

As Birdie and Mama got ready to leave, the cat ran toward the door like he wanted to come along. Birdie reached down to stroke his side, running her hand all the way up his bent tail. She nuzzled her face into him. "I'm sorry I can't take you. Stores have silly rules like no shirts, no shoes, no service. And no pets."

Foot Mart and the T. K. Much in the strip mall were already closed for the evening. But they had two hours until the ritzy mall closed, so that was where they ended up. Birdie had never been to Valley Lake's nicer mall, despite being friends with Hailey. This was because Hailey only shopped there with her mom. And now Birdie could see why.

The price tags were as fancy as the clothes. The silver glittery tights Hailey had worn with her jean skirt the day that everything had gone so horribly wrong between them were forty-five dollars. Birdie was shocked anyone would pay so much for something that still needed a skirt and a shirt to call itself an outfit. But she imagined Hailey's mom whipping her credit card out at store after store without a care in the world. A second ago a hundred dollars had seemed like so much money. But now she wondered if it was even enough to buy a proper gift for a girl like Hailey.

Mama held up a blue shirt. "What about this?"

Birdie shook her head. "Hailey wouldn't like it."

"I meant for you," Mama said.

"I don't want anything."

"What? Why not?"

"I want to spend all the money on Hailey. I really messed up with her, and I have to buy her something special—something amazing."

"But your shoes." Mama's eyes lowered to Birdie's worn sneakers.

Birdie shrugged.

"I insist you pick out some clothes for yourself," Mama said. "I'll buy it extra. I've noticed people staring."

Birdie hadn't noticed this, but then maybe Mama was more in tune with the subtleties of adult stares. Birdie was more accustomed to the kids at school who said mean things right to her face.

A woman who reminded Birdie of Hailey's mom clicked by in heels and soft fabrics. Birdie compared her to Mama, who was wearing one of her loud print dresses—a dress that looked like it had been dug out of someone's attic. If people were staring, they had reason to with Mama. "You need new clothes, too," Birdie said.

Mama nodded. "Don't I know it."

So, Mama and Birdie bought one new dress each. Birdie's was navy like Lily's, but instead of sparkly buttons, hers had a thin belt with a silver buckle at the waist. The sales clerk said the style was called a skater dress, though Birdie couldn't figure out what it had to do with skating. Nevertheless, it suited her, and most important of all, it fit. She also got silver ballet flats just like Lily's to match.

Mama bought a green dress that looked so nice on her that Birdie could hardly believe she was still her mama. Most of Mama's dresses incorporated every color in the rainbow. This might have been the first time, except for her maid's uniform, that Birdie had seen her in a solid color. Certainly, it was the first time she'd seen her in a brand-new mall-bought dress. And what a difference it made. Birdie swelled with pride. Her mama looked pretty.

Mama had the sales clerk cut the tags off the dresses so they could wear them around the mall, and the clerk seemed all too happy to aid in their transformation. At least she did until Mama asked her to put their old clothes into a fresh shopping bag. The clerk pinched each of their garments with two fingers, then poked them into the bag like they were an animal that might retaliate. This made Birdie feel awful, but as soon as they left the department store, it was easy to forget. She was in a new dress and new shoes, and her old self was hidden away.

They were ready to shop for Hailey in style.

They wandered around the outdoor part of the mall, breathing in the night air. For the first time since she'd taken the money from the gray house, Birdie relaxed. The mall felt safe, not like a place criminals or scary men in nuclear atom jackets might chase her. Fountains spouted cool water while statues of kids frozen in mid-air skipped with umbrellas. Birdie had the urge to jump into the fountain, but by some miracle, she stopped herself. If Kellog were there, she'd kick off her new shoes and do it, because he'd do it with her. Alone, Birdie didn't feel brave enough to jump into the ritzy mall's fountain where women like Hailey's mom clicked by wearing heels and tight lips. She wanted to call Kellog to tell him about all this, but she felt too bad about not sharing.

"Let's go find Jessie," Birdie suggested, suddenly remembering she knew someone at this mall.

"You're right. We should say hello," Mama said.

They found Jessie by the jewelry store looking crisp and official with his chest pushed forward and his hand near his weapon.

"Well, hello there, ladies," he said, relaxing and looking a little embarrassed, as if they'd caught him playing cops and robbers in his head. "What are ya'll doing here? Did you figure out who sent you that package? I promise it wasn't me."

"We know it wasn't," Mama said.

"I'm looking for a gift for my friend," Birdie cut in. "A really *nice* gift. What should I get her?"

Jessie rubbed his chin like he was really considering. "There's always jewelry, of course." He waved a hand toward the glassed display he was guarding, which featured a necklace with diamonds. The price tag read $3,300.

"Maybe not *that* nice. Any other ideas?"

"Well, what does she like?"

"You mean her hobbies?"

"Sure." Jessie nodded.

"Gymnastics."

"There's a dance store near Nordstrom."

"Really?"

"Girls your age ask me for directions to Putting on the Ritz all the time."

Suddenly Birdie remembered hearing Hailey and the other girls at school talk about this store, and without realizing it, she was sure this was how she'd come to call this mall the ritzy mall. "Thank you so much!" Birdie said.

"Put her there." Jessie stuck out his fist for her to bump, so Birdie touched her fist with his.

"Is there anything you might want, Jessie?" Mama asked to Birdie's surprise. "You've done so much for us, been so helpful whenever we've needed it, I'd like to return the favor."

"Are you kidding? You don't have to get me anything. We neighbors of Woodcroft help each other because it's the neighborly thing to do."

"Maybe a snack for your break?" Mama insisted.

"Really, you don't have to get me anything. Ya'll have fun, enjoy your shopping."

Mama put her hand on her hip like she wasn't taking no for an answer.

Jessie smiled. "Tell you what. There's a cupcake place next to Nordstrom. I've had my eye on a blueberry one with white frosting. Ya'll should check it out."

"We'll do that," Mama said, smiling back.

They found Putting on the Ritz and stepping inside felt like being trapped inside a glitter star. The multitude of costumes in shimmering sequins with bright explosions across the chests was blinding. Birdie didn't know Hailey's size, and after her own disaster with Lily's clothes, she didn't want to guess. She was feeling a little discouraged until she found a rack of batons. She picked up one with colorful flags on each end and gave it a twirl, circling her wrist around in a whirl. The ceiling of the shop was a giant mirror, and Birdie tilted her head to see the baton's flags take flight.

What a magnificent gift. The flags fluttered through the air, and Birdie imagined Hailey doing leaps and flips with the flags' colors flying around her.

She didn't think Hailey had anything like this, and in fact, when Birdie asked about it, the clerk—a woman with a wide smile and an equally wide bun swirled onto the top of her head and sealed with a wire dome—said it had just arrived. "It's an excellent choice," she assured Birdie. "And we have gift boxes for these." She pulled out a red baton-shaped box.

It was perfect.

The woman with the dome bun rang up the baton, but it came to $103.10—three dollars over budget. Birdie put her hands together in a silent plea to Mama.

But Mama was focused on a delicate barrette next to the register. "Look at these adorable hair ribbons."

Mama had lost her mind. Birdie's hair was too long and too thick to be held in place by something so small. Hair like hers needed a band of superhuman strength. "All I want is this baton for Hailey."

Mama sighed. "Okay. But that's a lot of money to spend on a gift. I'd rather you spent some of that money on yourself."

"I already got a new dress and new shoes."

Mama frowned but opened her purse to pay.

Birdie concentrated on the woman with the dome bun to see if she'd be surprised that Mama paid with two hundred-dollar bills. When they'd bought the dresses, the clerk hadn't cared, but the price of the clothes hadn't required so much change. Thankfully, dome bun didn't even raise an eyebrow. It was good to know that if you were dressed right, hundred-dollar bills weren't as rare a sighting at the ritzy mall as they might be in a poorer area like Polkville. Mama said it was important to use hundreds at the ritzy mall, where people wouldn't notice, so they had small bills later for things like laundry and newspapers.

Even the rosy-cheeked kid behind the cupcake counter who couldn't have been more than sixteen didn't bat a lash when Mama paid for only three cupcakes with a hundred-dollar bill. With new clothes, being a rich person had turned out to be easy. Birdie could get used to things being easy.

And she could definitely get used to eating cupcakes. Biting into crazy-thick frosting topping red, moist cake was pure heaven. She'd never had red velvet cake before. It was rich. She giggled with glee. She was rich.

Mama's face was covered in pink frosting and chocolate crumbs. She looked happier than Birdie had ever seen her. They were rich together, and it was sugar-high amazing.

21

Yet the next day, when Birdie put on her new dress to go to school, her *I'm sorry* present for Hailey tucked under her arm and her bookbag thick on her back with stacks of cash, Mama frowned. Maybe it was because the cat had gotten hair all over Birdie's nice dress. So, she brushed at the bright orange fur, the money on her back feeling like a lit fire.

"That dress is a bit fancy for school, isn't it?" Mama sometimes asked questions instead of telling Birdie what to do, but it was always easy to tell what Mama wanted to have happen.

"It's picture day," Birdie said, because it was.

"Don't you think it's a bit much even for picture day?"

Birdie shook her head. For once she had something nice to wear, and maybe if she was lucky, Mama would give her money to buy the pictures. And if she was even luckier, she'd escape the house before Mama noticed her overinflated bookbag.

But Mama's questions (that weren't really questions) continued. "Maybe you want to save your dress and silver shoes to wear outside of school?"

Birdie caught a glimpse of herself in the navy dress in the reflection of the living room's window. Minus her huge backpack, she looked so nice it took her breath away. She decided to argue. "What's wrong with wearing something nice to school?"

"People might ask questions, and I don't want you to have to lie." Mama eyed the shiny red box in Birdie's arms. "And won't Hailey think it's strange that you're giving her such a nice present for no reason?"

"You were standing there when I bought it," Birdie said.

"I know, but that was before I added minutes to my phone and called Dad." Mama paced the small length of the living room and chewed her bottom lip.

"What do you mean? What happened? What did Grandpa say?"

"Nothing. He's in the hospital, and he's too sick to talk on the phone."

"Oh." Birdie paused. "Is he going to be okay?"

"I hope so. But he didn't read my letter, which means he couldn't have known I needed money."

"How do you know?"

"His caretaker Karla said my letter is still sitting unopened on the table by his bed in the nursing home. And how could the return address be a local Ship It store, anyway? I assumed the package was from Grandpa, but I didn't really think it through."

"Oh."

"So now I'm questioning where this money came from. I called the Ship It store, but they don't know a thing about it. I don't know if Jessie robbed the jewelry store to try to help us or what is going on."

"What?! No! Jessie doesn't have anything to do with this."

Mama's eyes widened, and she gave Birdie a long look.

"Do *you* know something about this?"

"No," Birdie lied. "Jessie's just too nice to rob the place where he works. That's all."

Mama shook her head like she was knocking some sense back into herself. "Of course. You're right. He's a sweetheart. I'm just trying to figure out how one hundred and fifty thousand dollars arrived on our doorstep."

"God sent it. I prayed, remember?"

Mama put her hand over the giant daffodil on her dress like she was making sure she still had a heart-beat. "Honey. I hesitate to tell you what to believe because I want you to make your own choices. But I will say that I don't personally think life works like that. This money came from someone—an actual person. And until I know who and how they got it, I don't feel comfortable with you wearing that dress to school."

"But—"

"I don't want you getting into trouble."

"Trouble?" Trouble was resting on her back like thirty-five sticks of dynamite.

"I'm just imagining you telling everyone that you got to go shopping because a pile of money arrived like magic in the mail."

"I wouldn't say that."

"I don't want you to lie either."

Mama always thought twice about lying. She'd never lie up a storm like Birdie had. A guilty stomach-sick feeling stirred up inside Birdie. If Mama thought one lie might lead to trouble, what would she think about dozens?

"It's important that you listen to me on this, okay? The less questions people ask, the better off you'll be."

So, Birdie agreed then went to her room and changed out of her nice dress and back into the clothes of a poor girl. It seemed such a shame having new clothes and not being able to wear them.

"Can I at least have some money for the pictures?" Birdie asked, peeking into Mama's bedroom where

Mama sat staring at her phone. Birdie wasn't sure she actually wanted pictures of herself anymore, considering the only clean T-shirt she'd been able to find said, Wiener King: Home of the longest hot dogs.

"I need to use our small bills to do laundry. Until I break more of these hundreds, you'll just have to survive without pictures."

Birdie nodded.

"I'm going to make some phone calls. Have a good day at school." Mama gave her a kiss goodbye and closed the door to her room.

Since Mama wasn't looking, Birdie snuck back into her own room to grab Hailey's gift. She slipped out the door, happy she'd escaped with the two things that mattered: her *I'm sorry* present for Hailey and the rest of her and Mama's fortune. Even if that fortune felt like it might explode on her shoulders.

Birdie marched to the top of the school's stairs where the girls who had formerly been her friends chatted, waiting to be let inside.

Several of the girls shivered in their nice picture-day dresses, and Birdie guessed they'd opted not to ruin their look with a jacket. Of course Hailey had on the perfect coat. It looked almost like a dress itself. Birdie regretted that she'd been unable to convince

Mama to let her wear her new navy dress with the silver buckle. It wasn't too fancy. For once, she would have fit in. Instead she was wearing a Wiener King T-shirt and holding a long, hot dog–colored box.

But Birdie didn't turn back. She held out the gift and said in her biggest, boldest voice, "Hailey, I have a present for you."

The girls turned toward Birdie and confusion passed over a few of their faces, but Hailey seemed to understand and to recognize the box. "Is that from Putting on the Ritz?"

Birdie nodded. "I wanted to show you how sorry I am that I said what I did about your mom."

Hailey slipped off the ribbon. Resting the box on her lap, she lifted the lid, pushed the tissue paper back, and gasped.

Hailey looked touched. Then she squealed and grabbed Birdie into a fierce hug, and whispered in her ear, "You didn't have to get me a present," but Hailey smiled so happily. She took out the baton and spun it, rotating her wrist until the baton's flags twirled out. The other girls had to take a step back.

Murmurings of approval rose up from the lips of those who had shunned her. "Oh my gosh, it's so pretty!" Lily said.

"I want one!" Samiya cried.

"Look at the colors!" another girl, Birdie couldn't tell who, cooed.

The awestruck audience soaked in the wand's whirls and Hailey's cheer, and Birdie was given a new trial. Her jury reconsidered. And by the time the bell rang, she'd received a new verdict.

Exonerated and relieved, Birdie entered the school with her friends at her side.

At lunch she waited until the lunch lady's back was turned and raced into the cafeteria. She shoved her bookbag under the girls' table, not even bothering to wait in line for a lunch. Hailey asked Birdie to sit beside her, and she was surrounded by her friends again.

Lily offered her some pretzels, and the girls continued to admire Hailey's baton. "I saw this at Putting on the Ritz, but it was so expensive," Lily said.

"I emptied my piggy bank. You know, birthday money and stuff," Birdie lied.

Samiya looked impressed. "That's so incredibly sweet."

Hailey gave Birdie another hug. "You didn't have to spend all your savings on me."

The girls mashed together, their arms and shoulders bumping Birdie's, as they talked, laughed, and ate. Hailey's baton sparkled with the light, and Birdie was asked dozens of questions about it. How she had picked the flags' colors, the glitter; how had it all been put together. Lily said what a good job Birdie had done choosing it, and that she would like to get her own, but her mother had said she had to wait until next Christmas.

Birdie's battered sneakers bounced with joy as she floated through the rest of the school day. She fit in with the other girls in a way she hadn't before. She'd been able to talk about shopping and the things she'd seen at Putting on the Ritz and contribute something to the conversation. She'd gone the entire day without being called a bag lady or gaining a new nickname despite wearing a Wiener King T-shirt featuring an extra-long hot dog, which was nearly as big a miracle as finding a pile of money hidden in a wall.

When the school's photographer snapped her picture, Birdie smiled without even trying. And afterward, the photographer used his computer to edit out her shirt's ridiculous words and graphic. Below Birdie's winning smile, she looked like a regular girl wearing a plain, orange shirt instead of a poor kid who had to wear free T-shirts advertising oversized meat. And in her hand was an order form, if she wanted to get the pictures later. The best thing she could have hoped for had happened. Hailey was going to convince her mother to let them be best friends again. And she'd promised she would do it in time for the Winter Wonderland party on Saturday.

22

After school she went to the school library to look up the location of a different shipping store. Her backpack was still heavy with money that needed to be mailed to Mama, and as anxious as she was to be rid of it, she didn't want to go back to the Ship It store next to the laundromat. If she showed up there again, Travis or his dad might get suspicious, because how many packages could a kid her age need to ship?

So, she told the librarian that she needed to google some stuff for history class, and instead googled the next closest Ship It store. But according to Google Maps it was eleven miles away—too far for her skateboard.

She'd have to take a bus. She googled bus routes, wrote down the information, and stuffed it in her shoe so she wouldn't have to open her bookbag and reveal the hidden money to anyone who might be looking over. She really needed to ask Mama to buy her some pants with pockets so she didn't have to carry things in her sneakers.

Every time Birdie left the safety of the school building, she panicked. Her eyes always scanned for the man in the nuclear atom jacket. She imagined her days were numbered, and one day she'd find him waiting for her outside the school. Was today that day? Thankfully, no.

She made it home without issue.

"Mama!" Birdie raced into the apartment, excited to tell Mama that her friends were her friends again. But except for the cat, the living room and the kitchen were empty.

She went to her room to hide her money-heavy bookbag, then checked Mama's room. She wasn't in there either. Fear rose inside her like the lake in a heavy rain. What if the man in the nuclear atom jacket had come to their apartment? He could be holding Mama hostage so Birdie would give him back his money.

The cat meowed.

"Where's Mama?"

Cat would tell her if he could. He rubbed against her legs. She stroked his back all the way up to the tip of his broken tail and tried to calm down. She told herself she was being ridiculous.

Seconds later Mama flung open the door, carrying shopping bags. "Sorry I'm late. The lines at the mall were crazy. You'd think it was Christmastime instead of the middle of January."

Birdie rushed to give Mama a hug. "You went shopping?"

"I did! I bought you a new pair of sneakers."

"Really?!"

Birdie rifled through the bags Mama had set down until she found a shoebox.

"I'm sorry I didn't let you wear your dress and silver shoes to school. They're just so nice—I was afraid you would stick out. But I don't think sneakers will be cause for anyone to ask questions, do you? Even if they weren't cheap."

Holy moly. She couldn't believe it.

She was looking at a brand name that only Mama's newfound wealth could buy.

"Well, what do you think?" Mama asked.

Birdie lifted the lid and shrieked. There they were. The Vans shoes of her dreams. "Thank you! Thank you! Oh my god, thank you. You're the best!" She yanked off her ratty sneakers to put them on, but the folded piece of paper she'd written the bus schedule on fell out.

"What's that?" Mama asked.

"Nothing." Birdie snatched up the note, only without pockets she had nowhere else to hide it. She stuffed it under her leg.

"Nothing, huh? Since when does nothing look like a note from a boy?" Mama teased. "Tell me who he is. Don't keep your mama in the dark."

"Jacob. Jacob Powers," she blurted, surprising herself a little. *Did* she like him? Since he'd passed along her missed homework assignment, she'd been thinking nice things about him again.

"Is he Travis Powers's son?"

"Travis is his brother."

"Travis is also his father—owns the Ship It store on Yadkin Road. I should know, because I've talked to him enough lately."

Birdie's heart skipped a beat. "You have?"

"Well, yeah, I've called at least half a dozen times trying to find out who sent that package. I even went down there in person. But it was a cash transaction, so there's no credit card record. And Travis Sr. says he'd never have allowed a customer to use the store as a return address, but since Travis Jr. was working that day . . ."

"Is he going to get in trouble?"

"Who? Travis Jr.?"

Birdie nodded.

"He's a minor, not even on payroll. Just happened to be helping out that day while his dad did inventory."

Mama eyed the note under Birdie's leg. "You're too young for a boyfriend, okay?"

"Okay." She didn't really want a boyfriend—not like the kind Mama was talking about. She wanted someone to skate with, and maybe someone besides a cat she could talk to about criminals, hostages, and hidden money.

Mama ruffled her hair. "I need you to stay my little girl a while longer."

Birdie rolled her eyes.

"But you can be my little girl wearing new jeans and T-shirts." Mama handed her another shopping bag.

"You got me new clothes, too?"

"Just a few things I found on sale. The sales are incredible right now. I guess that's why everyone was out shopping." Mama eyed Birdie's feet, now clad in amazing black Vans. "Those shoes weren't on sale, though."

Birdie jumped up and threw her arms around Mama. "Thank you."

"You're welcome, sweetheart," Mama said, hugging her back. After she released her, Mama looked thoughtful. "I'm so baffled about where this money I'm spending came from. It has to be someone local. I talked to Jessie again, and I do believe he has nothing to do with it."

"I told you he didn't."

"The question is, who does? Mr. Powers asked his son, but he doesn't remember who came in that day."

Birdie let out her breath in relief. Travis hadn't ratted her out. Maybe he wasn't so bad after all. She pulled more new clothes from the bag. Awesome-looking jeans (with pockets!), two solid-colored T-shirts not advertising anything (yay!), and a *Thrasher* shirt (double yay!). She hugged them to her chest and looked up at Mama. "I love it all."

But Mama had a worried expression on her face. "I wonder if I should contact the police."

Birdie froze. "The police?"

"Yeah, I'm thinking about it. But, I can't imagine they would know where it came from any better than I do."

"You can't call the police!" Birdie shouted.

"I'm just thinking out loud here. I just want to figure this out."

"There's nothing to figure out. The money is yours, end of story." Birdie slapped her hand down hard on the coffee table.

Mama raised her eyebrows at Birdie. "Calm down. I know you like all the new things, but money arriving in a box from god knows where is weird, and I want to do the right thing."

Birdie shrugged. "It's not that weird." Not nearly as weird as finding half a million dollars in a wall.

Mama laughed. "I guess that's what's great about being a kid. Nothing is weird, because anything is possible."

"Anything *is* possible."

Mama laughed again. But she didn't look convinced.

23

Birdie had on her new jeans, her *Thrasher* shirt, and the most amazing Vans on the planet. Only this troubling feeling wouldn't let up. This feeling like everything she'd been working so hard for was going to come crashing down. Which didn't make sense. She should feel like a million bucks—or half a million anyway. She grabbed her skateboard and her bookbag with the sticks of dynamite that she couldn't wait to get rid of, and was about to head out the door to school, when Mama called her.

"Birdie!"

Birdie joined her. "Yeah?"

"Straight home after school." Mama tapped a page of

the newspaper and showed it to Birdie. There was a picture of two men. The headline read, PRISON ESCAPEES SPOTTED AT BISCUIT HUT IN VALLEY LAKE.

Birdie leaned in for a closer look at the mugshots. Neither of them looked like the guy in the nuclear atom jacket, but it was hard to tell. "Were these the criminals you were worried about in Mrs. Hillmore's neighborhood?"

"That's right. I thought they'd be long gone out of Valley Lake by now, but whoever wrote this article thinks they're still here. So, straight home after school, okay?"

Birdie nodded and ran out the door before Mama could see the panic in her eyes.

At school Jacob was the first to notice Birdie was no longer in danger of being arrested by the fashion police. "Nice Vans."

"Thanks." It was what she wanted—to have awesome clothes and get compliments—especially from Jacob, but this strange feeling came with it, like her sneakers changing how people saw her on the outside might also change who she was on the inside. And if she changed on the inside, who was she changing into? She thought about how she'd told that self-serving lie to Mama about not wanting new shoes, and felt guilty Mama had rewarded her with the shiny new Vans on her feet. She shifted her money-heavy backpack. She'd already changed. And she wasn't sure it was into someone she liked.

"I'm going skating after school with my brother if you want to come," Jacob said.

She hesitated. "Yeah?"

"Travis isn't so bad if you get to know him. He makes great skate ramps and—"

"It's not your brother. It's just . . . my mom wants me straight home after school." Jacob looked disappointed. He walked away fast—before she could explain. She almost called him back, but she didn't want to tell him about the prison break if she couldn't also tell him the escapees might be after her for their money. So, she let him walk away.

"Those shoes really suit you," Hailey said at lunch.

"They're cool," Lily agreed. "They'll look nice with those black jeans I gave you. Why haven't you worn them? I mean, those jeans you have on look great. I was just wondering." Lily didn't wait for an answer. Her arms raised in excitement. "Oh! I have this great shirt at home that would look amazing on you that I've been meaning to bring you."

"That's okay. You don't have to. My mom bought me some new clothes." She didn't need Lily's charity clothes anymore.

The girls changed the subject to the upcoming Biltmore Estate trip—who was going to sit on the bus with whom. And Birdie's heart soared when it was decided that she and Hailey would sit together. But her stomach clenched when Hailey brought up her Winter Wonderland party. Birdie might not be sitting next to anyone at that because she wouldn't be there.

"The whole neighborhood is coming. Mom says she wants it to be even bigger than last year. And we're going to get a fake snow machine for the backyard and hang snowflakes and lights in the trees. If the weather's warm enough, we're going to eat outside. It's going to be so pretty."

"Have you asked your mom if I can come?" Birdie ventured.

"I did. We had a huge fight, but she says you can."

"What?! That's amazing! How did you convince her?"

"I told her I don't care what she thinks—we're going to be friends no matter what."

"Aww!" Birdie threw her arms around Hailey's neck.

When she released her, Hailey said, "She also wants you to come home with me today after school."

Birdie paused because while she'd been over to Hailey's house after school before, she'd never been specifically invited by Hailey's mom. "Why? I mean, not that I don't want to come over, but I—"

"She says she wants to talk to you."

Birdie gulped. "What about?"

Hailey shrugged. "She wouldn't tell me."

Huh. This was odd. Birdie got an in-trouble feeling like she'd been asked to Mrs. Alvarez's office again.

"Do you think it's about the lake?" Was Mrs. Kirkland going to scold Birdie for being a bad influence on her daughter—making Hailey cross the lake and fall in—even though Birdie had done none of these things?

"I'm sorry. I really don't know," Hailey said. "Just come home with me after school, and we can find out."

24

Birdie met up with Hailey after school. "I just need to run by the front office to call my mom. To tell her I won't be home."

"Here, call her on my phone." Hailey passed Birdie the kind of phone that had internet, played games, made videos, and did who knew what else. "It's insane you don't have your own phone," Hailey sympathized. "I mean, sorry, I know you can't afford it, but *still*. How does your mother survive?"

"Don't you mean, how do *I* survive?" Birdie asked.

"No, I mean *your mother*. Mine doesn't know how to function if she can't get ahold of me every second of the day."

Birdie shrugged. Her mother wasn't like Hailey's. Her mother trusted her. "We just manage somehow."

After it had all been arranged, Birdie tangled up into Hailey's mother's car, clutching a Pilates mat that was in the seat between her legs. Birdie wasn't sure if Mrs. Kirkland hadn't made room for her in the seat on purpose or if she'd just forgotten Birdie was coming home with Hailey. Birdie had a feeling, though, that Mrs. Kirkland wasn't the type to forget things.

Well, what else was there to do but get through this? Birdie took a deep breath. "Good to see you, Mrs. Kirkland. Thanks for letting me come over." She wanted to add a thanks so much for letting her and Hailey be friends again, but maybe it was better not to bring it up. She wasn't sure what Hailey had done to convince her mom to change her mind, but she *was* sure Mrs. Kirkland could change it back again at any moment.

Hailey's mom was always either *going to* or *coming from* Pilates. So as usual, she was dressed in expensive-looking spandex. Today, her muscles rippled through loud fabric featuring a neon tiger with his mouth open. The tiger turned to face Birdie in the back seat. "You're welcome any time I can be home to keep an eye on you girls."

"Thank you," she replied to Mrs. Kirkland, trying to sound as grateful as she was.

All she needed was her friendship with Hailey. Still, it was tempting to tell Mrs. Kirkland that she wasn't a bad influence just because of where she lived, and that in fact, she and Mama were rich now. So rich that they had enough money to move out of Woodcroft Apartments, and heck, maybe they'd move next door to the Kirklands. Or better yet, they'd build an even fancier neighborhood with a giant gate and a guard who didn't let in any riffraff, no sir. And boy, wouldn't Hailey and her mother be lucky if they were allowed inside. Oh, not to worry, Birdie would be sure to tell the guard to open the gate for the Kirklands. But not just anyone would be able to drive through where Birdie and Mama would live. All this threatened to spill forth from her mouth. But she'd learned her lesson about saying whatever angry thought popped into her head. She smashed her lips together hard for the rest of the car ride.

At Hailey's house, Mrs. Kirkland offered the girls fresh-baked cookies. But Birdie had sense enough to refuse. Mrs. Kirkland's cookies were vegetables in disguise, featuring ingredients like carrots or zucchini. Mrs. Kirkland was one of those moms who thought everything should be healthy, even dessert. Luckily, Birdie had some buckeye candies in her backpack. She tried to psychically communicate this to Hailey, because she didn't mind sharing. And after a few eye flashes, it seemed to work, because Hailey said no to the cookies, too.

"Let's go," Hailey said. "I want to show you all the tricks I can do with the baton you got me."

"About that—" Hailey's mom interrupted, her voice stopping them with its commanding tone.

So close. They'd nearly escaped.

The baton rested in Hailey's hand, the flags blowing lightly as Hailey waited for her mom to speak.

"I don't think we can accept such a nice gift."

Hailey looked surprised. "What do you mean?"

"I mean, I think you should give it back to Birdie."

Hailey stared down at the baton, but made no move to return it.

"Hailey," her mother said in a warning tone.

"I bought it for Hailey, Mrs. Kirkland," Birdie jumped in. "We got into a fight, and I wanted to make things up to her."

"I know, but we can't accept something so . . . expensive."

Yes, it was expensive. But Hailey had gotten expensive presents from her other friends at Christmas only weeks ago. Lily had given her a gymnast charm necklace that Birdie knew for a fact was made of real gold, because she'd seen the 14k tag hanging off the clasp. It didn't make any sense, unless it had something to do with Birdie herself.

Birdie stuck out her chin. "I can afford it, if that's what you're worried about."

"You can?" Mrs. Kirkland's eyes grew wide as if she realized that what she was asking wasn't very polite, but the question was already out there, hanging in the air demanding an answer. An answer better than Birdie emptying her piggy bank and spending every dime of her birthday money.

"My grandfather . . ." Birdie paused because she didn't want to lie, she really didn't, but Mama was right. The truth was too weird for words. "My grandfather sent us some money." And she could have left it at that, but she couldn't resist the opportunity to let Mrs. Kirkland know that she didn't need to worry anymore that her daughter was friends with a poor girl. "He passed away. He left us some money in his will . . . lots of money." Piles and piles of money, she wanted to shout.

Mrs. Kirkland's face darkened. "Oh, I'm so sorry. I didn't realize."

Hailey gazed at Birdie sympathetically. "I'm sorry, too."

"It's okay," Birdie said, trying to lighten the mood. "He was old. It was his time." She'd heard someone say this about a woman who used to work at the Polkville Post Office.

"Are you going to have to miss the field trip for the funeral?" Hailey asked. The field trip to the Biltmore Estate was tomorrow.

"Oh, no," Birdie said. "Mama wouldn't want me to miss the field trip."

Mrs. Kirkland gave Birdie an odd stare, and Birdie realized she'd said the wrong thing, but she hadn't thought about missing days of school for a fake funeral. This was the problem with lying. You told one lie, and then you had to think up another, and before you knew it, you were caught.

And Birdie was definitely caught.

Mrs. Kirkland's eyes didn't release her. "Why don't you go start your homework." She continued looking at Birdie even though she was talking to Hailey. "I need to talk to Birdie alone."

Hailey checked her phone for the time. "Don't you have Pilates?" Pilates was the only thing that tore Mrs. Kirkland away from hovering over her daughter, and Hailey looked forward to it almost as much as she did the Summer Olympics.

"No, I went earlier today so I could be home with you girls," her mother said. "Let me talk to Birdie alone for a minute, okay?" Mrs. Kirkland put out her hand for the baton.

Hailey's mouth dropped open slightly, but despite Birdie's pleading eyes, Hailey gave her mother the baton and left Birdie alone in the kitchen.

Mrs. Kirkland tapped the end of the baton in her opposite hand a few times like a teacher might tap a ruler. And after what seemed like a decade of staring deep into Birdie's eyes, she asked, "Did your grandfather *really* die?"

Birdie nodded, deeply regretting her choice for a lie.

Mrs. Kirkland continued to eye her and tap the baton. "When did he die?"

"Last Sunday." Birdie shifted her backpack uncomfortably, scanning the room for something that might save her. She willed the microwave to ding or the burner to set fire, but nothing moved. Even the beautiful blown-glass clock the Kirklands had gotten on their trip to Venice appeared to be out of batteries, its usual ticktock stilled.

"And when did you get the inheritance money?"

"The next day."

"It just doesn't add up." Mrs. Kirkland shook her head. She paused. Silent for what felt like an eternity. "Are you sure there isn't anything you want to tell me about how you got this?" She held up the baton.

Birdie shook her head and stood so still she thought she might turn to stone.

"Okay, then," Mrs. Kirkland said, like the matter was far from settled. "I'll be right here in the kitchen, waiting for you to change your mind. If you like, you can even write me a note explaining everything and slip it into my hand before you leave."

Birdie remained statue-still.

Finally, Mrs. Kirkland told her she could leave, and Birdie flew out of the kitchen so fast she slammed her elbow on the doorframe. When she got to Hailey's room, she was hugging her arm and trying not to say all the bad words racing in her head.

"What did she want?" Hailey asked, her voice urgent. "Why did she want to talk to you?" She whispered since the kitchen, where no doubt Mrs. Kirkland was eavesdropping, was just next door.

Birdie whispered back, "Your mother doesn't believe in rags to riches." While it was true that Birdie had been lying to Mrs. Kirkland, and obviously Birdie wasn't very good at it, the truth was no more believable. Poor girls didn't find money in walls and suddenly become rich. Poor girls didn't have money for expensive gifts. It just didn't happen like that. What was far more likely was that Birdie was a thief.

"What?" Hailey whispered frantically. "Ugh, why doesn't she leave? I wanted us to sneak out to Vivian's."

Vivian's Vintage was a store located way back near school. Birdie didn't know how Hailey thought they would get there from here. But Hailey had it all worked out. She pulled a credit card from her purse and smiled. "I downloaded the Ryde app. Now we can order a car and go wherever we want. Lily and Samiya are scared to come with me, and anyway they don't like vintage. So, I'm super glad we're friends again." Hailey gave Birdie a warm smile, and it felt good. Really good.

But Birdie shook her head. "We'll have to find something else to do." There was no way Mrs. Kirkland would leave her daughter alone with a thief.

It was never going to happen.

Not for a billion dollars and not in a billion years.

25

There was no doubt that Mrs. Kirkland was suspicious of Birdie, but the question was, what would she do about it? Birdie didn't want to stick around to find out. When Mama came to pick her up from Hailey's house, she couldn't get to the car fast enough. She just wanted to be home in her own room with her own mother nearby.

But home sweet home had a police cruiser in the parking lot with its lights spinning and an actual police officer standing outside their apartment door. Birdie and Mama shared a startled look.

Had Mrs. Kirkland really called the cops on Birdie because she thought she'd stolen a baton? Or worse, the police were there to take her money away?

Jessie stood outside his apartment with the door open.

"The police better not be messing with Jessie." Mama ran over in a panic. "Is everything all right?"

An officer stood next to Jessie with a clipboard. "Did you hear anything unusual last night around nine?" the officer interrupted.

"No, we sure didn't," Mama said.

The officer eyed Birdie's bookbag like he could see right through it to the truth. But after an awkward pause, he seemed to decide he didn't care to talk to a kid. "Okay, well, we'll do what we can to monitor the area." He didn't look any of them in the eye, which gave Birdie the impression he would do no such thing. The police didn't generally waste their time over at Woodcroft.

"What happened?" Birdie asked, needing to know if it had anything to do with her and Mama's money.

"My apartment got broken into while I was at work last night," Jessie said with a shrug like it was no big thing.

"You mean someone stole all your stuff?" Birdie shrieked, because she didn't know anyone who'd been robbed, and it seemed like a big deal to her. A super big deal. Because what if the man in the nuclear atom jacket had gotten the wrong house? He might have meant to rob Birdie's.

"No, no. Didn't take much. Just some meat I had in the freezer and twenty bucks I had in a drawer. Made a real mess while they were at it, but hey, my place was already a mess, so no harm done. I'm just happy the poor, hungry soul got some food."

"There's a real kindness in you," Mama said.

It was true; Jessie's generous nature never failed to surprise Birdie. If someone stole her and Mama's food, she'd be mad. Madder than mad. Or she would have been, before she and Mama were rich. Before she had bigger problems than someone taking a little bit of food.

"We could lend you some money for groceries if you need it," Birdie offered because she knew what it was like to have an empty pantry. She hadn't exactly had to go hungry before she and Mama had found the money, but another few days, and it might have come to it. Maybe Jessie didn't have to pinch pennies like her and Mama, but she had a feeling he probably did. No one at Woodcroft had money to spare.

Jessie smiled at her. "Now who's the one with kindness in her heart?" He patted his oversized belly. "Don't worry about me, Little Bird. I've been storing up food for the winter. High time I used some reserves."

Jessie went back inside his apartment, and once Birdie and Mama were safely inside theirs with the door closed, Birdie still couldn't shake the feeling that the man in the nuclear atom jacket had tried to hunt her down.

Mama must have been worried, too, because she ran to her room and came back with the cash.

She proceeded to put it in a Ziploc bag.

Birdie sat at the kitchen table with the cat in her lap. She tried to calm her nerves by rubbing the cat along his back to the tip of his crooked tail the way she liked to do.

Mama put the Ziploc bag of money in the freezer.

Birdie paused her hand in mid-stroke over the cat. "What are you doing?"

"Putting this money in a safe place. I'd hate for it to get stolen if our apartment got broken into."

They'd recently watched an episode of *Let's Go Home* where someone said only a moron didn't keep "cold cash" handy, meaning money hidden in the freezer. It was a popular show. Everyone and their grandmother had probably seen it. It almost felt after watching that episode, that the freezer would be the first place a burglar would look. How could Mama think this was a safe spot?

"Why don't we put it in the bank?" Birdie suggested since that was the place normal people kept their money. The bank would be the safest place.

"I'd like to, but I can't deposit so much money at once without the government wondering where I got it. I didn't earn this money. I've got to pay taxes. It's a whole mess that I've got to figure out." Mama shook her head.

"Do you think the burglars were looking for *our* money, and they accidentally got the wrong apartment?" Birdie couldn't keep the worry to herself another minute.

Mama raised her eyebrows at her. "How in the world would anyone know we had this much cash? Did you tell someone?"

Birdie shook her head. She couldn't tell Mama that the criminals who'd escaped from jail might be looking for their money.

"You really can't tell anyone we have this much money in our apartment, Birdie. I don't want us to get robbed."

Birdie didn't want them to get robbed either. The money needed to be protected. "What if we paid Jessie to guard it? Jessie has a gun and experience guarding things."

Birdie had set her own bag of money at her feet under the table. Her back was killing her from carrying it around everywhere.

"Jessie can't sit here 24/7 guarding our money. He has to go to work. It'll be just fine in the freezer. Did you finish all your homework?" Mama eyed Birdie's bookbag.

Birdie shook her head.

"Looks like you have a lot. Go in your room and close the door, because I'm going to watch the news in a bit."

Mama always made Birdie leave the room when she watched the news. She didn't want Birdie to see all the crime and injustice that went on in the world. But Birdie could hear Mama get upset when they showed the police shooting or beating up innocent people just because of the color of their skin. Mama had a tendency to talk to the TV as if it could hear her.

Birdie had an idea. "Can you drive me to the library? I need to do some research for a history project. You can drop me there and pick me up when the news is finished?"

Mama paused and then she nodded. "Okay. They're always so nice there. It was almost worth moving here just to have such a beautiful library."

Mama was right. The Valley Lake Public Library was gorgeous. It had big, floor-to-ceiling windows that let in lots of sunlight. That evening the yellow-and-orange sunset splashed across the tan bean bag chairs in the enormous children's room. The books always seemed brand-new as if they never got checked out, and the bathroom sparkled like no one ever went in there. The public library in Polkville had been too small for a children's room, the books were well loved, and the bathrooms always stank of body odor. Birdie didn't really like to read, so she had only gone there if she needed the internet. It struck her as odd that both libraries were public yet seemed so different—like her Valley Lake school versus her Polkville school—but she guessed that was the point of moving to Valley Lake.

She plopped herself into one of the comfy bean bag chairs and tried to think, but the librarian kept looking over at her. She wore a cutesy, flared dress with books on it that contrasted sharply with a snake tattoo slithering down her arm. Despite the snake, the woman kept smiling at Birdie like she wanted to be best friends.

The other problem was that the library was near empty. There was an older boy with a laptop at the table, but other than him, the children's room was deserted. Still, Birdie carefully opened her bookbag full of money and dug around for the bus schedule she'd copied.

Wait a minute. This schedule was no good. She was in a different location.

The computers were thankfully facing away from the librarian and the boy. But instead of looking up the bus route from the library like she'd planned, she typed in the address of the house where she'd found the money: 4945 Lakeshore Drive, Valley Lake, NC—just out of curiosity to see if something came up.

Several headlines appeared.

LAKE HOUSE INVESTMENTS
TOO GOOD TO BE TRUE

ARREST MADE IN
REAL ESTATE SCAM THAT
PREYED ON THE ELDERLY

RESIDENTS OF EVERCREST
TESTIFY AGAINST MEN ARRESTED
FOR SCAMMING THEM

As she read through the articles, an ice-cold sweat broke out on her neck and trickled down her spine.

26

Was God *really* Robin Hood—taking from the rich to give to the poor?

It sure seemed like it, because the men who had lived at 4945 Lakeshore Drive had talked old folks—most of whom lived in Evercrest—out of their money through a lake house real estate scam. But what the news didn't know was that they'd then hid the money in the wall of their house, where God or the cat or fate had shown it to Birdie.

The next morning Birdie chewed her lip instead of her cereal.

She'd barely slept, tossing the information she'd discovered at the library over and over in her mind. Deep down maybe she'd known the money had to come from somewhere. But the thought was buried so deep she'd never stopped to consider from whom.

Well, now she knew, even though she wished she didn't. The money in her bookbag belonged to Evercrest's elderly residents—people the men from the gray house had befriended then swindled. The articles hadn't listed any names, but Birdie wondered if grouchy old Mrs. Hillmore who got Mama fired was one of them. She wouldn't want to take money from sweet, old ladies, but maybe she might not mind taking money from someone like Mrs. Hillmore.

Before she left the library, Birdie had looked around, taking in the library's pristine couches, expensive computers, and those big, beautiful windows. Valley Lake was so wealthy. There was money everywhere she looked. Shouldn't she and Mama have a little?

Rich people had more money than they needed. They weren't in danger of getting kicked out of their big houses or not having enough money for groceries.

She knew Kellog would agree with her, and suddenly, she needed him to.

Mama was still getting dressed, so Birdie had time. "Mama, can I call Kellog? I keep forgetting to call him back."

"He's probably sleeping, but okay," Mama said.

Birdie snatched up Mama's phone and dialed. She stepped outside the apartment onto the concrete landing for privacy.

When Kellog answered, she said, "Do you want to hear a crazy story?"

"Does it explain why you haven't been returning my phone calls and why you're calling me so early in the morning?"

"It does," she said.

"Okay, I'm listening."

"You know how when I saw you last, I had diarrhea?"

"I've tried to forget your bowel habits, but yeah, I remember."

"Well, what would you say if I told you that I didn't have diarrhea. That instead, I had a bunch of hundred-dollar bills stuffed into my pants?"

"I'd say your pants are on fire! You big liar."

"You're right that I'm a liar, but this is the truth, and once I convince you, you're probably not going to speak to me anymore for keeping it all from you. So, I should probably tell you now that I love you, and I'm sorry."

Kellog was silent for a few seconds. They weren't the sort of family that said *I love you.* "You're scaring me."

"Those holes in the walls of that house were there because someone was looking for the half a million dollars that I found."

There were several more, long seconds of silence. Finally, he said, "There's no way you could fit half a million in your pants."

"I went back for the rest the next day. I skipped school, snuck back to the house, and filled up my bookbag with stacks of hundreds. Then I mailed some of it in a box to Mama so she could have it."

"You're serious."

"Yes."

"That's ridiculous. Why wouldn't you have shared it with me?"

"I didn't want Mama to clean houses anymore."

Kellog's voice rose. "It was half a million dollars. I think you could have spared a few thousand."

"I know. I could have, and I'm sorry." It was cold outside, and Birdie hadn't put on her jacket. She shivered.

"Are you calling to give me some of it, then?"

"Yes. But I found out the money is stolen. The guys who lived in that house scammed a bunch of old people out of their retirement savings."

Kellog didn't say anything for a long beat.

She stared at the different colors of brown paint on the outside of the building.

Finally, he said, "Well, that sucks."

"Rich folks—they all lived in Evercrest. You saw those houses. People like that have so much money they probably hardly noticed they lost any—nobody's going without food or anything."

Kellog paused. "Yeah, probably not. But how do you know? Old people can't work. They need their retirement."

"I just know, Kellog. Geez. Come on, I thought you'd be on my side. I thought you'd be excited for me to send you a box of money. I mailed Mama hers from the Ship It store. So, how much do you want me to send you?"

"All of it?" He laughed. "Kidding. I don't know. Fifty percent. Fifty, fifty send it in a jiffy."

"Did you just make that up?"

"I don't know. Maybe. Or I might have heard it somewhere. Nobody's after this money, are they? Can it be traced?"

Birdie's mind raced. "I don't think so. There might be *someone* after it, though. My next-door neighbor's apartment got broken into. This guy saw me take the money from the house, and I think he's after me."

"Are you serious right now? You're over there living some kind of high-speed chase movie?"

"Do you think I should call the police?"

"Whoa! Nobody said anything about the police."

"You think I'd get in trouble for taking the money?"

"No . . . I don't know. Just never call the police if you can help it."

"Do you think I shouldn't have taken it?"

"I probably would've. All the cash? I'd have taken some of it for sure."

"But you acted like it was a bad thing to take money from people. It was a mean, old rich lady in Evercrest who got Mama fired, you know."

"I know. And I know if you call the police, they will keep that money you found. Guaranteed. Those old people will never see it."

"Yes, they will." But suddenly Birdie wasn't sure. "Why do you think that?"

"It happens all the time. The police are crooked."

"You're making that up. You don't know."

"Where's the money now?"

"I'm carrying it around on my back every day—in my bookbag."

"Well, that's super stupid. You should hide it."

Mama stuck her head out the front door. "You ready?"

"I gotta go, Kellog."

Birdie hung up and went back into the house. She thought she'd feel better calling Kellog, but now she felt worse than ever.

27

Mama looked like a million bucks in her new mall-bought dress.

"You look really nice, Mama. That's a great outfit for the Biltmore House." Birdie was happy Mama had something so spectacular to wear on the field trip.

"I'm sorry, honey. I'm not going to be able to go with you."

"What? Why not?"

At Birdie's old school in Polkville, no one wanted to be the baby who had his or her parent along on a field trip. But at Valley Lake Elementary, all the popular kids' moms came, even if there were already enough chaperones, and people actually felt sorry for you if your mom couldn't come. Birdie's mom had never been on a field trip with her because Birdie's mom always had to work. But now, Mama didn't have to work, and Birdie desperately wanted her to come.

"I already called the school. They have so many parents coming that they said they didn't need me. So, I'm going to the library."

"Why do you need to go to the library? We were just there last night."

"There's a lecture on making good investments, and I want to learn. I also want to ask if anyone knows how to pay taxes on money given as a gift."

"But I wanted you to see all the costumes from *Downton Abbey*," Birdie begged. Mr. Gladwell had promised there would be costumes from Mama's favorite TV show on display at the Biltmore, and she really wanted Mama to see it.

"You can tell me all about them when you get home." Mama turned in her new green dress so Birdie could zip her up.

"Can I have a few dollars for lunch? Mr. Gladwell said we'd stop at a fast-food place on the way."

Mama opened the freezer and pulled out the Ziploc bag. She peeled off a hundred-dollar bill from one of the stacks and handed it to Birdie.

Birdie had to try one last time to get Mama to protect their money. "Burglars probably know to check the freezer. Maybe you should stay home . . . to guard it."

"Birdie, really. I'm not going to sit here all day in case a burglar comes. And anyway, if one did, what would I do, hit him over the head with my shoe?" Mama laughed, but Birdie didn't think it was funny.

"Look, I know you're scared because Jessie's apartment got broken into. But Jessie's got the day off work and he and some other neighbors have started a neighborhood watch. And I looked up the crime statistics in Valley Lake before we moved here, and they're the lowest in the state. So, I have to believe this robbery is a rare incident that won't repeat itself. But when I get back, maybe I'll have a better idea for where to keep this money. Because I do feel silly keeping it next to the peas and carrots."

Birdie eyed the cold hundred-dollar bill between her fingers. "Are you sure you don't have anything smaller?" She didn't think she should try to spend a hundred-dollar bill without Mama there.

"I used up all our small change doing laundry and running errands."

Everything they owned had been dirty, so Birdie could see how this might have happened.

"But what's everyone going to think about me having a hundred-dollar bill?" Even Hailey didn't go around with hundred-dollar bills in her pocket. Hailey's mom already thought she was a thief. All Birdie needed was everyone else thinking she was, too.

"We'll stop and get change on the way," Mama said.

"Okay, but when can I just tell everyone we have money? Hailey's mom doesn't believe I can afford a baton," Birdie blurted.

"What? I wanted us to return that baton to the store. Did you give it to her even though I asked you not to?"

"Yes."

"Birdie." Mama drew out her name in a groan.

Birdie hung her head.

"Well, I guess I'm the one who let you buy it for her." Mama folded her arms. "What happened?"

"Nothing." Ugh, here she was having to lie again. Why couldn't she keep her mouth shut? "Mrs. Kirkland is just giving me funny looks, so I wanted to be able to tell her we have money now . . . when can I do that?"

"I guess you can tell her Grandpa sent us money even though I can't see how he did it from the Ship It store down the street. And I can't imagine he actually has that much money to be sending us, since his caretaker told me he hasn't paid her in two months. Honestly, I think he's broke. He's just the only person I've been able to think of who *would* send us money."

Why hadn't Birdie kept it simple like this? Now she had Mama's permission to say the money was from Grandpa, but she'd gone and made a mess by saying he died. She had to learn not to say more than she needed to.

At least she was doing a good job keeping quiet about some things—like the fact that she might be living a cops and robbers movie. The burglar was probably looking for her and Mama's apartment. And he might come back. The guy in the nuclear atom jacket didn't look like the type to give up. Kellog was right. Birdie couldn't keep lugging the money around everywhere, breaking her back, panicking every time anyone looked too hard at her. It couldn't stay in their apartment at Woodcroft either.

No. Money this big belonged at a rich person's house.

She concocted a plan. A bonkers plan because she was essentially going to have to do it right under Mama's nose. "Can you drop me off at Hailey's house instead of at school? I just realized I left my sweater over there. Her mom can drive us to the bus pickup."

They'd been up before dawn because the chartered bus would leave before school started to make the long drive to the estate. Hailey had trouble waking up at school's regular time, so Birdie was counting on her running at least a few minutes late. "Can I borrow your phone to call her?"

Mama passed Birdie her phone. "Why don't you just ask her to bring you your sweater?"

"No, no. I'm not sure where I left it, and Hailey is terrible at finding things."

Hailey answered on the tenth ring, and it was clear from her mumbled hello that she'd still been sleeping. "What time is it?"

"Time to go as soon as I get there. I forgot my sweater over there. Wait for me, I'm coming over."

"What? You did? Okay. Sure."

Birdie hung up and handed the phone back to Mama. "See? Hailey's dad thinks alarm clocks are bad for your heart, so they're always oversleeping. Hailey wasn't even awake yet."

"If she's not ready, aren't you girls going to miss the bus?"

"Mrs. Kirkland's one of the chaperones, so they can't leave without us."

"Okay, well, let's go then."

Birdie headed out to the parking lot with Mama, but as soon as Mama opened the car door, Birdie stopped. "Oh no! I forgot my books."

"I thought you didn't have class today."

"I don't, but I wanted to study on the bus. Stay here. I'll be right back." Birdie ran toward their apartment.

She grabbed her bookbag full of money, then ran for the kitchen. She flung open the freezer door and considered whether or not she should take Mama's "cold cash," too. Ultimately, she decided she'd better leave it where it was. Mama might need it or freak out if it was gone. She slung her bookbag on her back and raced for the car.

Mama eyed her bag. "Good grief. How much homework are they giving you now? Your bookbag has been loaded down for days."

"A lot. A bunch of tests coming up that I need to study for." Birdie tried to crush the bag beneath her feet to make it look smaller, but it only caused her knees to rise awkwardly to her chest.

Mama started the car and backed out. "Maybe I should talk to your teachers about not scheduling all your tests at once. You're too young to have so much homework. Kids are supposed to have fun and enjoy their field trips."

"No, Mama. Seriously. It's fine. I don't mind."

Mama gave her that impressed look again. The one where Birdie was some big hero. And she tried to tell herself that by protecting the money for her and Mama, maybe she was.

She was making sure Mama could afford to send her on fun field trips. Though, technically, this one had been paid for by Mr. Gladwell.

Birdie smiled.

Not anymore. She had the money to pay Mr. Gladwell back.

At Hailey's house, Birdie kissed Mama goodbye and flew out of the car as fast as she could while carrying a bookbag with, oh, just shy of half a million dollars. She stood on the porch like she was waiting for Hailey to open the door, only she hadn't rung the bell. She waved frantically to Mama trying to get her to leave.

Finally, she did, and only seconds later Birdie realized they'd forgotten to stop and get change. Great. Now she was stuck with a hundred-dollar bill for lunch. Well, there was nothing to be done about it, and she had a bigger problem to solve.

Free from her mother's eyes, she ran to the back of Hailey's house, climbed the treehouse ladder, and found the trapdoor. She took out the Taboo game to make space and placed the thick stacks of cash deep inside the hole. She placed Hailey's blanket on top, and then she shut the trap lid door.

28

The entire car ride to school, Mrs. Kirkland wouldn't stop asking Birdie if she had something she needed to talk about—as if Birdie had come over so unexpectedly that morning to confess to being a thief. Hailey's mom had even demanded complete quiet in case Birdie decided she had something to say. Hailey wasn't allowed to talk, and music was off-limits. So, they'd ridden to school in utter silence. A silence Birdie would have been happy to break if she'd known what to say to make Hailey's mom leave her alone.

As soon as the car stopped rolling, the girls leapt out. They ran like track stars to where their classmates were clustered around the big charter bus that would take them to the Biltmore Estate.

Lily spotted the girls and waved them over. "Come see Samiya's ring. It's to die for."

Now everyone was gathered around her staring at the ring on her hand.

Samiya's mom stood beside her daughter in a rich, pink shirt. It had tiny mirrors embedded in the fabric that flashed when she moved.

Samiya laughed nervously as the kids gathered around to get a look at her ring. She seemed like she was embarrassed to have caused such a fuss. The ring had what looked like real diamonds in a figure eight around two bigger-looking diamonds.

"Is it real?" Birdie blurted, because she'd never seen a ring with so many diamonds before.

Samiya nodded, lowering her eyes. "It was my grandma's. I didn't even know her that well, but she left it to me in her will."

"That's lucky," Jacob said. "I knew my grandmother super well, but she didn't leave me anything when she died."

Birdie leaned over Samiya's hand to get a closer look. "It looks great on you," she said only to be polite. She actually thought the large jeweled ring would be better off in a museum than on Samiya's finger. Sure, Samiya's mom wore clothes that might be nice enough for diamonds, but Samiya wore jeans and T-shirts. If it were Birdie's, she'd sell it for money.

"What an amazing coincidence!" Hailey jumped in. "Birdie's grandfather just died, and left her an inheritance." Hailey innocently spread the lie that Birdie had told.

Birdie flashed Hailey a hush-up look.

"Was it a secret?" Hailey looked startled, like she had failed her friend's trust without meaning to.

"It's okay," Birdie reassured her, trying to look sad, like mentioning her dead grandfather was the problem. Only it wasn't. The lie she'd told was making a pest of itself.

Samiya smiled at Birdie sympathetically. They both seemed to silently agree they hated being put on the spot.

"I'm sorry about your grandfather," Samiya said. "Were you close?"

Birdie shook her head, thankful Mr. Gladwell was now clapping his hands and herding them onto the bus.

"Give me the ring so you don't lose it," Samiya's mother insisted, holding her hand out toward her daughter.

"Mom! Grandma left it to *me*, not you. She thought I was old enough to be responsible for it. And you said I could wear it on special occasions." Samiya closed her hand around the ring and moved it away from her mother's grasp.

"That's before I realized it's still too big, and it's going to fall off. We need to get it resized again. Put it in your purse. Zip it in the inner pocket so it doesn't fall out." Samiya's mother looked exasperated, like the two of them had been fighting about this all morning.

"Mom, stop worrying. I won't lose it." She touched Birdie's shoulder. "Do you want to sit together?"

Birdie caught Hailey's hand and clutched it tightly. "I'm sorry, I already promised Hailey."

"It's okay, I don't mind," Hailey offered. "I can sit with Lily." Lily stood nearby and perked up at this turn of events.

"I . . ." Normally, Birdie might be excited to sit with Samiya. When she gave her presentation on Hinduism, Birdie had been amazed. No one else at Valley Lake was Indian or a Hindu, and Samiya didn't seem to care one bit. She hadn't seemed nervous at all. But Birdie had a bad feeling Samiya intended to ask her more questions that would require lies for answers.

Hailey let go of Birdie's hand. Samiya grabbed it, and Birdie found herself led away.

"Did you miss days of school? Is that why you brought your bookbag? When we went to India last month for my grandmother's funeral, I had a hard time catching up on all the work."

Instead of money, Birdie's bookbag now held the Taboo game from Hailey's treehouse. She hoped Samiya couldn't tell it wasn't books. She decided she was probably safe and was about to repeat the lie she'd told Mama about all the tests she had coming up. But Samiya didn't wait for a response before she fired the next question.

"What happened when they read your grandfather's will? You should have seen my brother's face when they told him our grandma left him a sitar."

Birdie didn't know what that was, but Samiya immediately told her so she didn't have to ask.

"It's this crazy, huge musical instrument. It's bigger than he is. What was your grandfather's funeral like? Being near a dead person is super creepy, right?" She shivered and dragged Birdie onto the bus. Birdie looked longingly toward Hailey who had chosen a seat at the front, while Samiya pulled Birdie to the back, directly across from Mrs. Kirkland. The short car ride with her that morning had been bad enough. She was about to protest, to suggest they sit somewhere else, but the only other available seats were singles. Samiya's excitement about dead bodies had cost them choice seating.

29

Birdie's one little white lie about her grandfather dying grew into an elaborate tale involving a billion-dollar chocolate fortune and her grandfather rolling out of the casket when an unsuspecting pallbearer tripped on a pair of missing false teeth.

Birdie had used her long-ago discarded idea of selling buckeye candies to spin the tale of her grandfather's wealth. A humble baking business that developed into a multimillion-dollar fortune through the simple power of Birdie's imagination.

Birdie knew her story was over-the-top and didn't make much sense, but she'd gotten caught up in topping Samiya.

When the bus turned onto the long tree-lined drive-way to the estate, Birdie finally noticed Mrs. Kirkland staring at her like a hawk on its prey. So, she shut up and stared out the window. The word *driveway* was a vast understatement, because Mr. Gladwell stood at the front of the bus booming that it was three miles long. Birdie couldn't imagine how much candy a person would have to sell to afford such a driveway, never mind the grand house that stood at the end of it. After a few minutes of staring out the window at the trees, waiting for the driveway to end, she looked back at Samiya. Quiet tears rolled down her friend's round cheeks.

"Are you okay?" Birdie whispered.

Samiya shrugged and looked down like she was embarrassed.

"Are you upset about your grandmother?"

Her friend nodded. After a minute Samiya said, "I was just thinking about these stories she used to tell. I can't remember what they were about. They were soooo long"—she stopped so her chest could heave—"and boring—like so, so boring, and I didn't pay atten-tion. I'd play video games with my brother and try to tune her out."

Birdie put her arm on Samiya's hand and squeezed.

"Why didn't I listen? Maybe now I'd think they were interesting." Samiya burst into a fresh set of tears.

Birdie slid closer and put her arm around Samiya. "Don't you think your brother or your mom might remember? Could you ask them to tell you?"

Samiya sucked back some snot running out of her nose. "I guess. That's a good idea. Mom probably does. Still, it's not the same as hearing her tell them again."

"Yeah."

Samiya laid her head on Birdie's shoulder and they were quiet for a bit. "Do you imagine your grandfather not being there for holidays?"

"I used to see him more when my grandmother was alive, but now it's usually just me and Mom at Christmas. My dad's not around."

"Oh, I'm sorry," Samiya said.

And Birdie almost wanted to tell her the truth—that her dad was in prison and that she hardly knew a thing about him. But that countless times she'd imagined how great it would be if everything was different. If he could sit next to her and Mama as they opened their presents, grinning when they liked the gifts he'd gotten them. "Sometimes we get together with my aunt Laura and my cousin Kellog, and that's nice. But a lot of the time my aunt has to work. Lots of people go out to Tubby's for steak dinner on Christmas."

Samiya wiped her tears and giggled. "Tubby's?"

Birdie nodded. "That's what's written on the sign— right next to the cow in a bell. Polkville folks love it. No one seems to care that it actually makes you tubby, because they have an all-you-can-eat dessert buffet— ice cream, cookies, brownies. It's insane. Come to Polkville with me, and I'll take you. Aunt Laura gets me a discount."

Samiya nodded like she was really going to come. "I'll go anywhere for all-you-can-eat ice cream."

A silence fell over the bus as the mansion became visible through the trees. Birdie had thought, finding that great big pile of money, that she and Mama were rich. But she saw now that *this . . .* this was rich.

Jacob stood up on his seat. "It's enormous! You weren't kidding around, Mr. G." Everyone laughed.

Mr. Gladwell smiled. "When it comes to the facts, I don't kid. And I'm also not kidding that you have to sit in your seat until the bus parks."

Jacob sat. "Sorry, Mr. G."

The line to get inside the estate went all the way down the massive set of stairs and into the garden. Mr. Gladwell had said this was the largest privately owned home in the United States, and judging from the line, here seemed to be the entire country wanting to pay forty dollars to see it. So, this was how the rich stayed rich—they charged admission to their homes. If that big pile of money Birdie had found wasn't a secret, maybe she could charge a money-viewing fee. She could see the billboards now: Just three dollars to see what half a million dollars in cash looks like!

People everywhere were taking group photos with their phones, posing in front of the Biltmore and its perfect mountain backdrop. Jacob and Aiden were doing thumbs-up and making goofy faces.

"Do you want to take a picture together?" Hailey asked, interrupting Birdie's thoughts of making money off money.

"Sure," Birdie said as she, Lily, and Samiya gathered around Hailey for a photo.

Hailey handed her phone to her mom to take the picture, but Mrs. Kirkland paused.

"Birdie, can you move a little to the left? I can't see Hailey."

Birdie was on the end. She unwrapped her arm from Hailey's shoulder and moved over a few inches.

"Just a little more," Mrs. Kirkland said, waving her farther away from Hailey.

What was going on? Was she knocking Birdie out of the picture?

With picture taking finished, Hailey took back her phone. But she must not have liked what she saw, because she grabbed Birdie and stuck out her arm to do a selfie.

She showed Birdie the shot. It was a good one, and Birdie wished she had a phone, too, so she could take pictures to bring home to show Mama. More than that, she wished Mama were there to see everything in person. They weren't even inside yet, and everything was already as awesome as Mr. Gladwell had promised. The only thing that wasn't awesome was Mrs. Kirkland.

"Your mom is terrifying," Birdie said once they'd rejoined the line. "She still hates me so much."

"Too bad. You're my best friend. She has to get over it." Hailey looped her arm into Birdie's, and Birdie's fears melted.

As long as she and Hailey were friends, everything with the universe would be okay. And she couldn't let Mrs. Kirkland ruin this awesome trip.

The girls clustered together in the line. "This house looks European. Don't you think?" Hailey asked.

"Like straight out of England," Lily agreed.

"Imagine playing croquet on this lawn. How amazing would that be?" Samiya said.

"Totally amazing," Birdie lied, because she had no idea what Samiya was talking about. She hadn't been to Europe or played croquet. But maybe now that she and Mama were rich, they should go somewhere. How luxurious would that be to fly on an airplane to Europe?

"I think it looks like the castle of a god," Jacob said, appearing behind them. "Like maybe Zeus's from *The Lightning Thief.*"

"That book is so good," Samiya said.

"It really is," Lily agreed.

"What do you think, Birdie?" Jacob looked at her. "Could this be Zeus's house?"

"Of course," Birdie said, like she knew what she was talking about. She hadn't even heard of the book, much less read it. She didn't usually read books outside of school assignments.

"Here are your tickets." Mr. Gladwell handed each of them their admissions ticket, working his way down the line to Birdie.

On the bus she had made a plan to borrow money from Samiya at lunchtime so she didn't have to use her hundred-dollar bill. But now, in her excitement to pay Mr. Gladwell back—her excitement not to be such a charity case—Birdie didn't think.

She whipped out her hundred, and Mr. Gladwell's eyes enlarged at the sight of such a large bill in the hand of such a small girl. Too late, Birdie realized her mistake.

"You don't have to pay me—" Mr. Gladwell's eyes lingered on the bill.

Mr. Gladwell hadn't been expecting her to pay him back.

"Here, just take it," Birdie insisted, wanting the bill to disappear and the lingering eyes to linger elsewhere.

"Well, okay, but you really don't have to."

"I insist."

He pulled out his wallet and proceeded to count out twenties.

It was on the tip of her tongue to tell him to keep the change. But of course, overpaying by eighty dollars (half off for children!) would be absurd. The change itself, though, was making a scene, because Birdie had to squash and fold the twenties into the small pocket of her jeans, where they sat in an uncomfortable bulge because she'd left her backpack on the bus, and she didn't own a purse like the other girls. All the while, Mrs. Kirkland watched, her eyes like high beams on Birdie's neck.

"Where'd you get your purse?" Birdie asked Samiya. Samiya's purse was an over-the-shoulder bag with a patchwork of bright colors.

"On my India trip." Samiya smiled and took it off her shoulder for Birdie to see.

It felt heavy in her hands, and Birdie wondered what Samiya was lugging around, so she opened it.

Inside was enough makeup to impress Aunt Laura. "Wow, you have a lot of makeup. My mom won't even let me wear lip gloss," Birdie confessed. If Birdie's lips were chapped, Mama made Birdie dip her finger into the giant tub of Vaseline from the medicine cabinet. Birdie had never been that interested in makeup, so other than wanting to try a bubblegum-flavored lip balm she'd seen once—more out of curiosity about the taste than a need to get done up—this was mostly okay.

But maybe it wasn't okay that she didn't have a purse, a place to put all her newfound money. Instead she had to hide half a million dollars in a treehouse and shove way too many twenties into her pocket.

The impressive exterior of the Biltmore was matched only by the 250 rooms on the interior. Birdie followed the crowd through the house, peering over the red velvet ropes into bedrooms, sitting rooms, dining rooms, and ballrooms. Mannequins were dressed in clothes from *Downton Abbey*. The figures wore beaded gowns and tuxes with tails, their arms and legs positioned as if talking, playing the piano, or having a dinner party.

But despite the mannequins' lifelike display, it was hard to think of the Biltmore Estate as a house. Even *mansion* didn't seem quite the right word. The idea that a regular family had once lived there sounded like one of Birdie's lies. The house had its own library with 23,000 books, an indoor swimming pool, a bowling alley, and even a place for the horses to exercise indoors so they didn't have to go out in the cold. She tried to imagine her and Mama living it up in such a place, but she couldn't get past the image of them shocked and gaping, afraid to touch anything.

They were stopped at the library now. Stacks of beautiful hardcover books encircled a room so tall that a twirling set of stairs reached a second-floor landing, where the books continued on from there to the ceiling. A woman behind the rope was telling a story about George Vanderbilt, the rich guy who'd created the library and everything else in this enormous house.

"George had a secret passageway built to the second floor so women could sneak down in their nightgowns to grab a book to read before bed. Women weren't allowed out of their rooms unless they were fully dressed, you know. But George wanted people to take advantage of his library. Be sure to look for the staircase when you go to the second floor now, okay? It's roped off, and it's one of the few parts of the house no one's allowed in, not even me, but I wanted you to know it's there." She smiled conspiratorially.

Hailey leaned over to whisper into Birdie's ear. "I want to see that. It sounds cool."

Birdie agreed. There was something about the secret staircase that made the house finally seem real—like a place where people like Birdie and Mama could live. Birdie squeezed her mind to picture Mama in one of the elegant gowns, a red one with fine lace and a ribboned waist. For herself she chose a white gown with crisscross straps and black lace. It took all the powers of her imagination, but there they were, she and Mama in their finery, relaxed and reading by the fire.

Anything was possible, right?

All these people believed it, too—this crowd of folks most of whom had paid forty dollars to see what it might be like to be buck-wild crazy rich. Regular people taking a day away from their regular lives to see the most spectacular American dream that had ever been realized. Regular folks, nothing special about any of them, except one.

A man in a nuclear atom jacket.

30

Birdie's mouth went as dry as the pages of those hundred-year-old books. She was sure it was him—the man outside the gray house in Evercrest who'd yelled at her to stop. And there he was, looking her way.

She briefly thought to tell someone: Mr. Gladwell, Samiya's mom, some capable adult. But what would she say? That a man was following her, perhaps in order to kidnap her so he could take her money?

The crowd in front of her was thick with bodies. She pushed toward the red velvet rope, trying to get around the people. She wanted a bathroom, a closet, a place to curl into an invisible ball.

"What's wrong?" Hailey had appeared at her side.

"I don't like that guy," Birdie sputtered, which made no sense at all. But Hailey took Birdie's arm and expertly led her through the crowd, as if the words *Get Me Out of Here* were flashing across her head.

Birdie followed Hailey until they could no longer see their classmates. She was too scared to think or care about where they might be going. But Hailey led her to the second floor as if she knew. Hailey wound her way this way and that until she found the secret passageway the woman in the library had mentioned.

It had a red velvet rope stretched over the entrance—the Biltmore's dignified no-trespassing sign. But Hailey was a girl used to getting what she wanted despite the rules, and she stepped across the rope as if it were an outstretched arm.

Birdie followed, the fear of the man from the gray house too palpable in her mind for good judgment to have a prayer.

They tucked into the secret hallway far enough that no one would find them. But beneath her feet, Birdie felt the floor change. No longer level, it dipped and sagged in a disturbingly unstable manner. For the first time, Birdie considered where she'd trespassed. "Is this safe?"

"You know, old houses." Hailey shrugged, like safety could hardly be expected. She grabbed Birdie's arm and pulled her close, her voice an urgent whisper. "Who was that guy?"

"Oh, him." Birdie's mind clamored for a lie. "A friend of my mom's. I didn't feel like saying hi."

Hailey watched Birdie, a deep distrust etching into her face. "You're not telling me the truth."

"I know. I'm sorry. It's just—it's a really big secret, and I'm not supposed to tell."

"You can't tell your best friend?" Hailey looked a little horrified. "I thought we told each other secrets. I thought we told each other *everything*."

"We do . . . usually. I swear. It's just this one time—"

"—the one time you have *a really big secret*—you can't," Hailey finished for her.

Birdie nodded.

"Fine," Hailey said, too promptly.

"Fine?"

"Super fine." Hailey flipped her razor-sharp hair and stomped deeper down the hallway, away from Birdie, probably hoping to find the exit.

And well, she found an exit all right.

Straight through the floor, her left leg punching through like paper. And here Birdie had thought she was done with gaping holes.

Three things happened at once:

1. Hailey's bloodcurdling scream.
2. A Biltmore alarm shrieking the beeping universally known to mean Intruder! Call the Police!

3. The hole crumbling open further as Hailey struggled to get free.

"Don't move!" Birdie shouted, throwing herself to the floor on her belly.

But Hailey panicked.

Birdie slid over and grabbed Hailey's hand. "Be still or you'll fall through."

"I need to get my leg out."

"Trust me. If you move, you're going to fall all the way through. I can see the next floor. It's a long way down." Through the hole was the Biltmore's library and a stack of red books the color of anger and regret.

"I don't want to be stuck in here."

"I know. Hold my hands."

In seconds, security was there, a stern-looking woman in uniform pulling Hailey out of the hole and to her feet on solid ground. A bunch of other security people joined seconds later. Birdie and Hailey were carefully led back down the treacherous hallway. Once it was determined that the girls were uninjured, the guards' voices raised in complaint about unmonitored kids and what a shame about all this damage to such a fine historic home.

"What's happening? Are you girls okay?" Mr. Gladwell's face was concerned instead of angry.

"I'm sorry, we—" Birdie began, the lie about getting lost interrupted.

Next to her Samiya shrieked and shrieked again, nearly as loud as the alarm that had blessedly stopped ringing. She dug frantically through her purse. "My ring! I can't find my ring!"

31

Samiya's mother took her to the bathroom, where they dumped out all the stuff from her purse and went through everything over and over, but the ring was nowhere to be found. Birdie's classmates were now canvassing the Biltmore's every corner looking for it.

Instead of helping with the search like she wanted to be, Birdie was in the guest relations office with Mr. Gladwell, Hailey, and Mrs. Kirkland. It felt a little like being sent to the principal's office, only with silk-covered seats and a mountain view.

"I can pay you back for everything," Birdie promised a smartly dressed woman who'd introduced herself as Diane Patton—*please, call me Diane.*

"Pay *her* back?" Mrs. Kirkland shook her head. "She should be paying *us*. I'll have you know my daughter is a talented gymnast, and if her leg is injured . . ." She let the threat hang.

"The area was roped off, which means it's not open to the public—precisely because it's not safe." Diane turned to Birdie and smiled kindly. "And don't worry, we have insurance for situations like this. But how you girls got through that rope without an alarm going off is what I want to know. We should have been alerted right away."

"My daughter doesn't know anything about disabling alarms," Mrs. Kirkland said. She pointed at Birdie. "That girl on the other hand is a liar and a thief. First, she stole an expensive gift for my daughter. Now she's stolen a diamond ring. Search her. I'm sure you'll find it."

"Whoa there." Mr. Gladwell held up his hand. "You can't go accusing Birdie when we don't know what happened."

"Oh, I didn't mean to imply that the girls had disabled the alarm or stolen anything," Diane jumped in. "No, no. That's not what I meant. I only meant I need to check our alarm system, because something malfunctioned. I don't think it would be possible for the girls to have messed with it."

"Oh. Well, I just wanted to say that none of this was my daughter's idea."

"Well, she did cross a rope she wasn't supposed to, but perhaps she just lost her way," Diane suggested.

"Actually, Mom, it *was* my idea." Hailey spoke for the first time since they'd entered the office. She'd been staring at her hands, not looking at Birdie. She continued not looking at Birdie. "The guard in the library was telling us about this secret passageway, and I wanted to see it."

Diane's eyes widened.

Mrs. Kirkland looked stricken. "Honey, please don't protect Birdie like this. I know Samiya's parents might press charges for her stealing that ring, but Birdie will have to accept the consequences of what she's done."

"Now what's this about stealing?" Diane shifted forward in her seat, like maybe she was dealing with something more sinister than accidental trespassing.

"I saw Birdie looking in Samiya's purse," Mrs. Kirkland tattled. "She had it in her hand. I was right there."

Mr. Gladwell turned to Birdie. "Did you take Samiya's ring?"

"I just liked her purse," Birdie insisted. "I asked her where she got it. I didn't take her ring. I didn't even see it in there."

Mrs. Kirkland's voice raised an octave. "But you were looking."

"That's enough." Mr. Gladwell's tone was firm. "Birdie says she didn't take it."

"I'm telling you. You cannot believe this girl. The lies she told on the bus on the way here. My god, it would make your head spin. And what is she doing with a hundred-dollar bill? You don't get inheritances that fast."

Mr. Gladwell stood up. "Thank you for your time, Diane. We're truly sorry to have caused damage to this gorgeous building. If we come again, we'll have a chaperone for every child, and you have my word this will never happen again."

"About that," Diane said. "While I'm not going to press charges against such young girls, and believe me I could"—she eyed Mrs. Kirkland as she said this—"because damage to a historic building *is* a serious matter, I do ask that you not return."

"What? We can't come back? *All* of us?" Mrs. Kirkland's face went paper white. Apparently, she wasn't used to being kicked out of places.

"I think it would be best if you didn't. Don't you?" Diane asked. "It'll be easier for me to convince myself that your daughter just lost her way in this large estate, rather than remember she intentionally went somewhere she knew she shouldn't and caused who knows how many thousands of dollars in damages."

Mrs. Kirkland nodded, her face falling, the realization that her daughter might not be totally innocent seeming to dawn on her.

"Can I trust you to leave the grounds right away? I don't need someone to escort you?"

"We'll leave immediately." Mr. Gladwell ushered them forward, his hand firm and warm on Birdie's shoulder.

They joined the rest of the class outside. "We can't leave," Samiya panicked. "We haven't found my ring."

"Surely we can have a few more minutes?" Samiya's mom had her arm crossed over her stomach like the thought of leaving behind such an expensive family heirloom was going to make her lose her lunch.

"I'm afraid not. I promised we'd go straightaway." Mr. Gladwell waved everyone toward the bus. "Come on, kids. Time to load up!"

Birdie looked back one last time at the impressive house, its gargoyles reaching longingly beyond the rooftops, as if they, too, knew she'd never be back and were trying to stop her from leaving. But they wouldn't stop her. She would escape this place, and the man inside it.

Samiya's mom was also looking back, maybe trying to determine the odds of anyone ever finding a needle in such a large haystack. Of all the places for Samiya to lose her ring, a house with 250 rooms on 8,000 acres had to be the worst.

"I told you we should have put that ring in a safety deposit box until you were eighteen. Why in the world did I let you convince me to bring it today? This is my punishment for spoiling you." Samiya's mom spoke to her daughter, who looked like she was going to cry.

As the class lined up for the bus, Birdie watched Mrs. Kirkland march directly to Samiya's mom. They whispered something together, and then Mrs. Kirkland raised accusing eyes to Birdie. Birdie didn't have to have supersonic hearing to know what Hailey's mom had said. She also didn't have to be a psychic to know that Mrs. Kirkland wouldn't be the only one who thought she was a thief. Samiya's mom would believe she was, too.

Word would spread. Soon everyone would believe Birdie had taken Samiya's ring, and there'd be nothing Birdie could do about it.

She got onto the bus and sat down, relieved that at least she was leaving the man with the nuclear atom jacket behind. No matter what gossip Mrs. Kirkland spread about her, nothing was scarier than him.

32

Whoever you'd sat with on the bus ride to the Biltmore was who you were supposed to sit with on the way home. Everybody knew it. But Samiya was so upset about her ring that she had switched to sit with her mom, which was understandable, of course. That left Hailey sitting with Lily, as was expected, and Birdie sitting alone.

So, Birdie had an hour-long ride with nothing to do but think about how everything was such a mess. And that Hailey wouldn't have chosen to sit with her even if switching seats were expected. Birdie could tell because Hailey still wouldn't make eye contact.

For the first twenty minutes Birdie stewed. *How dare Hailey get so mad at her just because she couldn't tell her everything. And how dare Mrs. Kirkland call her a liar and a thief.*

For the next twenty minutes she looked out the window and wished she had something in her bookbag besides Hailey's game of Taboo. Not only did it need more than one player, it was technically not hers, and therefore kind of *stolen*? Of course, she planned to give it back.

So, okay it was *borrowed*. But good grief what if Hailey saw her with it? She didn't want to think what might happen. If Hailey had gotten this mad over Birdie not telling her everything about the guy in the nuclear atom jacket, imagine how mad she would be when Birdie couldn't explain what she was doing toting around Hailey's Taboo game in her bookbag?

The following twenty minutes a few things began to occur to her, like that it was true she'd been lying a lot lately—maybe lying more than she'd been telling the truth. And that *did* kind of make her a liar like Mrs. Kirkland had said. And she didn't think she was a thief, but learning that the money she'd found *was* stolen from actual people even if they *were* rich was complicating things. Rich people didn't need the money and her and Mama did, but did that make it right?

She wasn't sure, because when she thought about her and Mama not having money to pay rent, that felt wrong, too.

Regardless, Mrs. Kirkland thought she was the bad kind of thief, so it seemed unlikely she'd be allowed to attend the Kirklands' Winter Wonderland party.

When they arrived at the school and filed off the bus, Birdie found Hailey. "Will I see you tomorrow?"

Hailey turned away and tried to pretend like she hadn't heard.

Birdie persisted, refusing to be frozen out. She tapped her friend's shoulder and spoke louder. "Can I still come to your party?"

Hailey whipped around. "Nobody wants you there."

Birdie glanced toward Lily and Samiya to see if this was true, but they wouldn't look at her.

Her heart popped her open like her skateboard over a water balloon. She'd known Hailey would say she couldn't come. Why did it wreck her so much? She'd worked so hard to win Hailey's friendship back, and just like that it was gone.

Slip. Slice. Silence.

Jacob stared right at her like he'd already heard the story of how she'd taken Samiya's ring. Or was he just staring at her because he was still disappointed that she hadn't gone skating with him? It was hard to tell.

Birdie walked to Mama's car, tears in her eyes, her

head hung low. So low she didn't notice Mama rushing toward her.

"Birdie." Mama took her shoulders, surprising her from her thoughts.

"What's wrong?"

"Dad . . . ," her voice choked up. ". . . he passed. Grandpa is gone."

"What?" Had the lie she'd told somehow made it back to Mama?

Mama grabbed Birdie in a tight hug, like she was so distraught she needed comforting. "I got us plane tickets for next Saturday, but I'm too late . . . we're too late. The nursing home called. I wanted—" Mama spoke in Birdie's ear, then, to Birdie's horror, started to cry.

Mama was a rock. Birdie could count on one hand the number of times she'd known her mother to shed actual tears. Mama pulled away and wiped at her dripping nose.

Birdie didn't know what to say. Had she made him die by lying about it? She glanced back to her classmates, thinking she wanted to cry, too. Maybe she and Mama could have a good cry together. But first they needed to get out of there.

She put her arm around Mama and led her to the car.

33

The next day was Saturday, and Mama was still crying. Today was Hailey's party, and Birdie felt like crying some more, too, seeing as how she'd lost her best friend and been uninvited to her party. Plus, maybe by saying her grandfather had died, she'd actually killed him—which would make her a lot worse than a liar and a thief. It would make her a murderer.

But once Mama started crying, it was like she couldn't stop. She cried all through breakfast, until finally it was lunchtime, and Birdie was so worried she considered calling Aunt Laura for help. Just when she was about to, Mama sat up suddenly from where she'd been lying in her pajamas on the couch. "I want to use some of the money to give him a nice funeral."

"That's a good idea." Birdie planned to take the bus to the Ship It store first thing on Monday so she could mail Mama another package of cash. That way Mama would have enough money for anything she needed.

Mama wiped at her eyes. "I gotta pull myself together. I need to go buy today's newspaper." Mama left to get dressed.

But she was gone only a few minutes when her phone rang. Birdie picked it up off the couch and took it to her.

"Hello? Oh, hi, Maddie."

Maddie was Hailey's mom's first name, so Birdie tried to stay to listen. But Mama was getting dressed and shooed her out.

After a few minutes Mama came in and sat on the sofa next to Birdie, wearing only a bra and pajama shorts, her face half made up.

"That was Mrs. Kirkland."

Birdie nodded.

"Calling to say they're having some big party."

"The Winter Wonderland party?" Maybe Mrs. Kirkland was calling to say Birdie was invited after all. It was a long shot, but hey, a girl could dream.

"They were outside setting up all the tables and chairs, and Hailey got sad that you wouldn't be there.

She started crying, saying you're keeping secrets from her."

Birdie was too shocked to speak.

Mama gave Birdie a long look. "I understand you have things you don't want to share with Hailey. But Mrs. Kirkland said something worse happened on the field trip. Something I should talk to you about."

Birdie's stomach hit the deck.

Mama waited patiently as Birdie gathered her thoughts (and her guts off the floor).

"Samiya lost a diamond ring that her grandmother left her. Mrs. Kirkland—and probably everyone else— thinks I took it. But I didn't."

"Why would she or anyone else think that?"

Birdie shrugged.

"Are you going to tell me what happened?"

Birdie shrugged again. "She doesn't like me. Because of where we live, I guess."

"Hailey's mom thinks you stole a ring because we live in Woodcroft instead of Evercrest?"

Birdie nodded.

"I'm going over there right now to talk to her." Mama jumped off the couch like she wasn't even going to bother to get dressed first. "If that's what she thinks, she's going to say it to my face."

"Mama, wait. I . . . I don't think you should go."

"Why not?"

Because she wasn't telling Mama everything. She wasn't telling her she'd lied about Grandpa being dead (before he'd actually died) and lied some more to Samiya on the bus. And Hailey's mom was going to tell Mama these truths if she went over there.

"She's a snob, that's why. You're not going to change her mind."

Mama narrowed her eyes like she could change anyone's mind if given half a chance.

"And you're already upset about Grandpa."

"You're right about that. But we need to get this sorted. I can't have her thinking you stole something when you didn't."

"Why don't you let me talk to her?"

Mama paused. She seemed to consider this.

"I'll tell her I didn't do it."

"I'm not sure that'll be good enough. I think this nonsense with you and Hailey's mom has gone on long enough, and it's time for me to get involved."

Birdie imagined Hailey setting up tables and chairs outside. Outside where the treehouse was. "Do you think there'll be a lot of little kids at the party? Kids who might want to play in a treehouse?"

Mama tilted her head slightly. "That's a strange question. But probably. She told me the whole neighborhood was invited, and she was really stressed about Hailey being so upset in front of so many people. Why are you asking?"

Birdie scrambled for a lie but found a truth. "Mrs. Kirkland won't let anyone play in the treehouse anymore."

Mama stared at Birdie a long beat like she was trying to wrap her head around why Birdie would care about this. "Are you telling me everything I should know?"

Birdie nodded. Nodding was easier than words when you were lying.

"We need to get this mess straightened out first, and this time, I think I should go alone." Mama went back to her bedroom to continue getting dressed.

Birdie rubbed the cat's fur along his crooked tail and tried to calm down. "I'm in trouble, Cat. What should I do?" Her mind worked as fast as it could trying to figure out how she was going to get over to the Kirklands' to rescue her and Mama's money from the treehouse before some kid decided to play up there. She also tried to work out what she was going to do about the lies she'd told. Mama would be so disappointed if she found out those horrible things Birdie had said from Mrs. Kirkland rather than from Birdie's own lips. She had to come clean. She couldn't lie like this to Mama anymore.

She knocked on Mama's door.

"Yes?"

"Mama, I . . ."

Mama opened the door. "Yes?"

"I don't want you to go."

"Why not?"

"It's embarrassing." She'd chickened out.

Mama cocked her head like she was trying to figure Birdie out again. "It's only embarrassing if you did it, and you didn't, right?"

"Right."

"Okay, then let me get dressed so I can go get my newspaper, then get to the Kirklands' to try to fix this."

Mama closed the door again. Birdie sat back on the couch and buried her head in the cat's fur. If only she never had to face the world again.

A few minutes later Mama left, and as soon as the door closed behind her, Birdie sprang to her feet.

She grabbed her bookbag and her skateboard. She had to get over to the Kirklands', too, and somehow get back home again before Mama got back. She wrote a note for Mama saying she'd gone to Jessie's to bring him the trash in case Mama got back before her. Maybe if it took Birdie too long, Mama would think she was next door chatting. Jessie was fun to talk to, and Mama might believe that.

34

There wasn't much time. Birdie worried she was going to get caught. It was probably stupid what she was doing, but what choice did she have? She couldn't let some neighborhood kid strike it rich by finding her and Mama's half a million dollars hidden under the trapdoor of Hailey's treehouse.

She skated so fast, even with the wind whipping around her, she broke a sweat. But when she came to the busy road—the one she wasn't supposed to cross— she took her time. She stopped. She looked both ways before running across four lanes to arrive at Hailey's. Music and voices trailed over the tall wooden fence. It sounded like Hailey and her dad were testing out the stereo system for the yard.

Birdie had no firm plan for how she was supposed to sneak up to the treehouse while a party she wasn't invited to was about to go on below it. She couldn't just open the fence and walk in like she was supposed to be there when she'd been specifically told not to be.

The only thing she could do was hope Hailey and her dad would decide to go back inside the house. So, she tucked herself behind the neighbor's hedges and waited.

Luck was on her side, because it didn't take long for Birdie to see the caterers arriving at the front door, and a few minutes later Mrs. Kirkland called Hailey and her dad inside for taste testing. When all seemed quiet, Birdie creaked open the gate.

To her horror, not only were Hailey and her dad gone, but the treehouse was gone, too. And so was the huge tree with thick branches that the treehouse had been sitting on, along with the ladder she'd hoped to climb to retrieve her hidden money.

In its place was nothing but air and a flat tree stump reaching only a few inches off the ground. Birdie swung her arms out where the tree used to be, as if it were now invisible, and she could feel her way for the ladder— which was nuts.

But she just couldn't believe it.

How could it be gone? And was her money gone, too?

She stood there in a stunned stupor, her hopes and dreams that Mama would never have to work again axed.

She might well have been rooted there until nightfall, grown branches, and become a tree herself if she hadn't heard someone coming back outside. It woke her into motion and caused her to scurry to her hiding spot in the hedges.

She had to think. She had to find her money.

Mrs. Kirkland hadn't wanted them to play in the treehouse anymore. So, she'd probably been the one to take it down. Which meant most likely Mrs. Kirkland had Birdie and Mama's money.

The window to Hailey's parents' room was along the opposite side of the house. She hid her skateboard in the bushes, ducked, ran across the front yard, and threw herself through the thankfully still-unlocked window to Hailey's parents' room.

She fell to the floor louder than she would have hoped. She stood up slowly inside the room where not even Hailey was allowed. Not a single thing was out of place. There was a four-poster bed, a fluffy-flowered comforter, a perfectly matching rug with throw pillows, and the Kirklands' wedding photo was blown up on the wall. Birdie opened the closet.

The closet was as neat as the room. The clothes had been blocked together by color, whites, beiges, blacks, and blues. Loose items were placed in pretty wicker baskets lined up in the top and bottom of the closet. Shoes sat up on racks like they were on display at a museum. Birdie rifled through the wicker baskets, but all she found were soft scarves and expensive-looking purses. She went to the dresser and opened every drawer. But there was no money there either.

She heard Hailey and her parents' voices down the hall *oohing* and *aahing* over the food. Apparently, Hailey had gotten over Birdie already—mourned their friendship and moved on. She imagined the cranberry-orange scones oozing with butter that Hailey had bragged about, and was half tempted to sneak in when they went back outside and grab a to-go plate.

Laughter trickled down the hallway and longing punched her in the guts.

Of course, she didn't want a to-go plate. She wanted a to-stay plate—to be at the party herself laughing, listening firsthand to all the things that would happen, sipping tea and nibbling small sandwiches.

Punch. Punch. Punch.

It was bad enough that she'd wrecked their friendship. Standing there eavesdropping as Hailey and her parents laughed like they didn't have a care in the world when her and Mama had so many was torture. She had to hurry. She had to get out of there.

Against the Kirklands' dresser mirror was a large jewelry box with tiny drawers. She opened them. Inside were necklaces, earrings, bracelets, and one absolutely stunning emerald ring. Glittering green and surrounded by diamonds, it was almost as spectacular as Samiya's ring. Birdie pinched it between her fingers and wondered how much it was worth.

She couldn't leave here without Mama's money. But she didn't know where it was. Everyone already thought she'd stolen a ring. What would it matter if she actually did? Mrs. Kirkland had Birdie's money hidden somewhere. This was just making things even.

She wore her infamous fake-pocket pants— the ones with a tiny sparkly button still inside the only real pocket. She slipped out the button and set it in the tiny drawer where the ring had once been. The button was a symbol of a previous shame. She should have tossed it in the lake along with Lily's charity clothes and drowned that awful day at school right along with this one. These weren't the days for scrapbook keepsakes pasted into pages to look back on fondly.

These were days to be forgotten.

But first she had to get through this one.

Her pulse quickened as she tucked Mrs. Kirkland's emerald ring into the now-empty only working pocket in her pants. The one just big enough to hold a small fortune.

She could make her exit out of Mrs. Kirkland's

window. No one would ever know she'd been there. She'd get away with it. She knew she would. But she forced her feet back across the hall to Hailey's room. She owed it to herself to check.

Hailey's room looked as it always did—a mess. Birdie had heard Mrs. Kirkland complain that no matter how often the housekeeper came, Hailey seemed to destroy her room seconds later. Clothes and shoes were tossed on the floor and all over the bed; necklaces and bracelets littered the dresser from end to end. Every drawer in the dresser was partially open and spilling with sweaters and jeans. Gymnastics trophies, medals, and ribbons lined the walls. There was so much . . . stuff. She opened Hailey's closet and dug around a few minutes. Everything under the sun. Everything except a half a million dollars minus a cold hundred fifty thousand.

She pulled out a photo of Hailey, maybe four or five years old, in her gymnastics leotard, getting a hug from her mother. It was in a gold frame engraved at the bottom with, "You'll always be my little girl. Love, Mom."

Something compelled her to set the photo upright on Hailey's bedside table instead of shoving it back into the closet. Despite the rush she should have been in, something also compelled her to hide under Hailey's bed. She curled onto her side and tucked her hands under her chin. Her heart hammered loud in her ears. What was she doing? She had to get out of there. But fear and anxiety had wrapped her like a straitjacket. What was going to become of her? What *had* become of her?

Mrs. Kirkland's words echoed in her head as she stared at the photo. *A liar and a thief.*

This was who she was now.

But was it who she wanted to be? Mrs. Kirkland believed Hailey's falling in the lake was her fault— that she was a bad person because of where she lived. Wasn't it only people who could do wrong, not places?

From under the bed Birdie saw a bulletin board of birthday cards and pictures on the wall. She spotted a glossy photo of Hailey and her dad—a photo Hailey had chosen to pin up instead of throw to the back of the closet, because her dad was so awesome. He had one of those innocent smiles—open, approachable. Birdie thought of her own dad.

A thief who'd ended up in jail.

She could've gotten a decent father like Hailey had. A father who went to work and helped out, one who made treehouses and tucked her in at night. But no. Instead she had gotten a thief and near murderer, and she had never felt more thoroughly robbed.

Birdie crawled out from under the bed and stood up straight.

Blood rushed to her head and made it pound. Mama

had lost her job telling the truth, and she hadn't regretted it. Her integrity had meant that much to her. When Mama had gotten a box of free money in the mail, instead of keeping it and not worrying about where it came from, she'd thought about things like going to the police and paying taxes.

Birdie raced across the hall and back into Mr. and Mrs. Kirkland's room where she'd found the thing that did not belong to her. She went to the dresser, pulled open the tiny drawer, and faced her shame. The sparkly-silver button, really more flaky than sparkly from all her rubbing and praying. She swapped it for the ring, quick as lightning before she changed her mind. Then she left the room.

The hallway remained empty. The doorbell rang and voices floated up the stairs, yet her hand continued to rest on Hailey's parents' doorknob. The ring continued to glitter in her mind.

She could still do it. She could slip it back into her pocket. It would be so easy. No one would know.

But *she* would know. And the secrets and lies would continue. The secrets that had caused Hailey to uninvite her to the Winter Wonderland party. The secrets that had caused her to lose her best friend. The lies that made it hard for her to make new best friends with confident girls like Samiya.

Whoever dies with the most friends wins.

She was losing. Losing her friends' trust, Mama's trust, and now she'd lost their money. She removed her hand from the doorknob.

She would not end up like her father.

Mrs. Kirkland would not be right.

If she opened the Kirklands' bedroom door again, lying would be her past and her future. If she walked away, lying could stay in her past. Honesty could be her way forward.

She wished she could ask Hailey to borrow her cell phone. She wanted to call Mama and tell her everything right now. But she didn't belong there. She was an intruder, and she needed to leave.

35

The doorbell rang again and then again. The voices multiplied. The party guests were arriving. Despite this, Birdie risked being seen to run across the hall to Hailey's room rather than go back into the room with the ring. She couldn't go back in the room with the ring.

She quickly closed herself in Hailey's room and tried to calm her heart. She'd made it. Next to the window that she planned to climb out of, she noticed a small suitcase tucked into the corner, which was odd, because as far as she knew Hailey hadn't gone on any trips lately. Birdie rolled it over and propped it up to use as a step, but before she climbed up, she unzipped it.

And there, wrapped in Hailey's blanket from the tree-house, lay the crisp stacks of Birdie's money.

Relief flooded over her. She ran her fingers over the cash. She could give Mama everything now. She could hand her every bill and tell her the whole crazy story. How the cat had helped her find a pile of money hidden in a wall. How she'd gone to the Ship It store to mail Mama the cash and bought men's laundry from a lady who might make donuts. How the money might be from criminals who wore nuclear atom jackets and one of them might know where she lives. That the money had been stolen from rich folks who lived in Evercrest. It would be hard to tell Mama the lies she had told about Grandpa. It would be even harder to tell her all these truths about the money.

But she would.

Because she wasn't a liar or a thief.

Not anymore.

She didn't want to have to climb in or out of any-more windows. She didn't want to have to keep putting money in and out of her bookbag.

The money inside, the bag over her shoulder, she opened the window. But what she saw on the other side made her hit the floor like the world was on fire: stop, drop, and roll. Her chest moved frantically up and down as she lay on her side and stared at the legs of her friend's dresser where she'd rolled across the room.

The man in the nuclear atom jacket was out there—in the Kirklands' front lawn.

He'd either followed her or he was there for the party. Did criminals get invited to parties? No, of course, they didn't.

Which meant he was following her!

She laid low and crawled outside Hailey's door.

She had to get out of there, but her face ran into Mrs. Kirkland's legs.

"What are you doing?" Mrs. Kirkland stood over where Birdie was still crouched on the floor.

"I'm um . . ." Birdie looked up at the woman who had called her a *liar and a thief.*

She knew with certainty that there was a lie out there that could save her if she thought hard enough. But she wasn't going to. "I left something in Hailey's treehouse. I climbed in through the window to see if I could find it. I'm sorry. I shouldn't have done that." Birdie hung her head.

"You *broke* in?" Mrs. Kirkland seemed shocked. Like even though it was a poor-girl-lying-thief Birdie in front of her, she hadn't expected it.

Birdie the liar, the thief, *and* the burglar. Mrs. Kirkland was never going to let her be friends with Hailey ever again.

"You come with me right now." Mrs. Kirkland's voice shook, her anger lit with a ferocious fear.

She led Birdie through the house, looking for her phone.

"Are you going to call the police?" Birdie asked.

Mrs. Kirkland's hand gripped around Birdie's arm. "I don't know. All our guests are arriving, and I'm afraid it would make a scene. But believe me if we weren't about to have a party, I certainly would."

Birdie's heart tipped over on its glass shelf and shattered into half a million pieces.

Groups of people were gathered talking in the living room. Hailey's dad and the man in the nuclear atom jacket approached them as they headed through the dining room. The guy who'd been chasing her was coming right for her.

In her panic Birdie tripped on the leg of a dining room chair. She went down hard, the fall bringing Mrs. Kirkland down with her.

"Are you okay?" Hailey's dad gave Mrs. Kirkland a hand to stand up. And to Birdie's great shock her own hand now rested in the man in the nuclear atom jacket's.

But not for long. She pulled away and ran.

"You come back here," Mrs. Kirkland shouted.

Birdie paused.

"What's going on?" Hailey's dad asked.

"She broke in. Climbed through the window. Can you believe it? Come back here!" she shouted again.

Birdie trudged over. The people talking in the living room turned to watch the commotion.

Mr. Kirkland seemed to take note of his wife's fear. "She's Hailey's friend, isn't she? Kids do crazy things sometimes."

"No truer statement has ever been said," the man in the nuclear atom jacket jumped in.

Everyone laughed.

The man turned to Birdie since she didn't know the story. "My nephews got themselves mixed up in an investment scam. They stole millions of dollars, which is about as crazy as it gets."

Mrs. Kirkland nodded. "Every time I hear about that, I can't believe it happened right down the road on Lakeshore."

"What address on Lakeshore?" Birdie asked the man in the atom jacket, but of course she knew the answer.

"It's 4945, why?"

The doorbell rang again.

Mrs. Kirkland answered it.

"Birdie?"

"Mama?"

"Birdie! What are you doing here?" Mama pushed past Mrs. Kirkland to come inside.

Hailey walked in the room with Samiya and Lily. "Birdie? Did you come for . . . your book that you left over here?" Hailey's eyes went to Birdie's bookbag, heavy with money. They shared a look. A look that said that Hailey had rescued Birdie's money from the treehouse and was trying to cover for her. And Birdie could play along. With Hailey backing her up, she could get out of this mess or at least avoid the police. She knew she could.

"What's going on?" Mama looked at Birdie, her eyes a mixture of confusion and dread.

Everyone seemed to be waiting for Birdie to say something that would make everything make sense— something normal and expected like that she'd forgotten a schoolbook she needed and didn't want to interrupt the party so she'd done something dumb and climbed in a window. But her life wasn't normal or expected. Her truth didn't make that kind of sense. If she were unlucky, her truth could get her arrested. She turned to the man in the nuclear atom jacket and braced herself. "I um . . . I think I have the money that your nephews stole." She opened her bookbag wide enough for him and everyone else who was rubbernecking to see.

"I found half a million dollars hidden in a wall at 4945 Lakeshore Drive."

36

The room burst into a flurry of questions, all of which Birdie tried to answer. She spilled the whole story to the whole neighborhood, plus Mama who had such a look of shock and horror on her face it was all Birdie could do to keep going. The truth, the whole truth, and nothing but the truth.

"This is amazing," the man in the nuclear atom jacket said. "I'm Mr. Garrett, by the way." He stuck out his hand like Birdie was supposed to shake it, so she did. He pumped like Birdie was the most interesting party guest he'd ever met.

"You weren't following me? You're not mad that I . . . went in the house?"

"No, and you're not the first kid to skate in that pool. I wouldn't be able to count how many kids I've chased out of there." Mr. Garrett shook his head. "Man, this is wild. I can't believe you found this money. My nephews' prison mates couldn't even find it, and they beat the walls to death looking."

Mama's eyes widened. "The convicts who escaped? The ones in the news? Oh my god, I should have realized."

"Those are the ones. I thought for sure they'd been misled—that there was nothing to find—just another lie my charming nephews had spun. They preyed on older people—people who couldn't travel. Showed them photos of lake houses in Florida and convinced them to invest their retirement funds—promised big returns. They counted on the fact that folks wouldn't fly out to see for themselves."

Hailey leaned in, her eyes saucers of interest. "What's going to happen to the money now?"

"They're going to give it to the police, honey," Mrs. Kirkland said.

Mr. Garrett jumped in. "Well, I'd like to make sure it gets back to the people it belongs to."

"Do you have their names?" Birdie asked.

"I met most of them in court. My nephews stole a lot more than what you found if this is only half a million, but the money can be divided among the victims. At least give them back something."

Mr. Garrett seemed so kindhearted—nothing like the horrible criminal she'd imagined him to be.

"I hope you're not considering returning this money on your own without police involvement." Mr. Kirkland gave Mr. Garrett a worried look.

"No, I suppose not," Mr. Garrett said.

"I think we should do the right thing . . . whatever that is," Birdie found herself saying. "The police would give the money back to who it belongs to, wouldn't they?"

"I'll try to make sure they do," Mr. Garrett said. He paused, thoughtful. "Was the cat who showed you the money orange? Super friendly?"

Birdie nodded.

"Probably my sister's cat."

Birdie's heart seized. "Do I need to give him back?" Giving up her and Mama's chance at being rich was awful enough. Giving up the cat might break her.

Mr. Garrett waved his hand. "No. He needed a good home. I'm glad you found him. I had wondered what happened to him."

Happiness flooded her.

"So, wait a minute. You had all this money hidden in our treehouse? How did you get it from the dead tree? We had it removed yesterday," Mrs. Kirkland asked.

Hailey rolled her eyes. "Mom. You told me to go get my stuff before they took it down, remember?" Hailey turned to Birdie. "I knew the money was yours as soon as I found it. I was waiting for you to tell me what to do with it."

"*You* were in on this?" Mrs. Kirkland looked like if she had one more shock, she'd need CPR.

"No. Birdie didn't tell me anything." She glared at Birdie. "Which by the way, the next time you have a story this nuts, I better be the first person you tell!"

Before they went to the police, Birdie and Mama stopped by the apartment to raid the freezer.

Mama held up the frozen bag of cash and dropped it on the kitchen counter. It gave a loud *thunk*. "Easy come, easy go."

"Oh, Mama, I screwed up so bad," Birdie moaned. "I should've told you the money was stolen, but I didn't want to worry you. I know that doesn't make it right, but I really wanted to make things up to you."

"Do you think lying is a good way to make things up to me?"

"No." Birdie paused. Her heart ached. "Did I kill Grandpa by saying he died . . . before he died?"

"No, sweetie, you didn't. But I think you should always be careful what you say."

"From now on, I'm going to, Mama, I promise. I just wanted so much for us to be rich. I didn't want you to have to clean houses anymore. I wanted you to have a good life."

"I already have a good life." Mama paused. "You don't think I have a good life?"

Birdie shrugged, and Mama put her arm around her and kissed her head. "I have you, don't I?"

"But I messed up so much."

"That's true. But as long as you know it and try to do better in the future, everything will be okay."

Would it, though? "But how will we pay rent—all those bills?" She eyed the cat's empty food bowl. They needed so many things.

"I suppose I'll get a job eventually. And if I don't, well, we just take it day by day."

"I really wanted you to never have to work again."

"And what would I do with myself all day?"

"I don't know." Birdie thought of the staged mannequins at the Biltmore. "Throw dinner parties?"

"That sounds like work to me."

"Rich people have cooks and servers. I'm pretty sure they don't have to lift a finger . . . like on *Downton Abbey*."

"I'm not going to tell you being rich wouldn't be nice. But I don't want you thinking I need a boatload of money to be happy. For the most part, I really do like my life." Mama gave her the side eye. "Especially when my daughter tells me the truth."

Birdie's heart squeezed. "I'm always going to, Mama. I really am."

Mama asked Birdie to put on her mall-bought dress to go to the police station. Mama had hers on already.

"You really think we should wear dresses that we bought with stolen money?" Birdie asked.

"We don't have a choice. Appearances matter. That's why they make you dress up when you go to court. Like it or not, people judge you based on how you look."

Birdie knew it was true. "I don't think it's fair, though." She gave the cat a bunch of snuggles before she slid on the dress. After she had it on, she wouldn't be able to touch him.

"Well, a lot of times it isn't. Jessie said when he applied for his job at the Valley Lake mall, they put him through the ringer—kept asking him for more and more references and paperwork—asking him the same questions over and over. But after he was hired, when he mentioned the intense interview process to the other security guards, they said they hadn't had to do so much."

"Because he's Brown and they're white?"

"Afraid so," Mama said. "So, as hard as we might get judged for looking poor, it's nothing compared to what some people go through."

Birdie thought about that. Before she'd found the money, she'd never felt lucky, but maybe she was lucky to be able to walk into a police station as a white girl in a nice dress. Maybe they'd go easy on her. Even if she might not deserve it.

They met Mr. Garrett in front of the Valley Lake Police Station. He wore his nuclear atom jacket like usual, and Mama asked him what the symbol meant.

"Oh, I teach high school physics. But I took a leave of absence this year to deal with my sister's house and sort out some things."

After a minute of small talk, they all walked in together. Birdie gripped Mama's hand and didn't let go—not even after they were seated and in front of an officer who was ready to listen. A pool of sweat between her and Mama's palms had formed, which caused Birdie's hand to threaten to slip free. She interlaced their fingers. She gripped harder. Was all this sweat hers?

Yes, of course, hers. Every last drop. She sipped in a tiny breath of air. She'd been holding her breath. Maybe if she held it long enough, she'd pass out and wake up at home.

Mr. Garrett and Mama were doing the talking, but suddenly, they stopped. Everyone stared at Birdie. The station's fluorescent lights made the officer's pale face ghastly. Like a zombie ready to bite a chunk of her.

If she weren't holding her breath, she may have run.

Mama turned to her. "Birdie, can you tell the officer everything that happened in your own words?"

The air she'd been holding exploded out of her with a sharp *pah.*

The officer who was going to take her statement frowned like he hoped Birdie didn't take a long time building up her nerve.

Mama could tell the story herself. It would come out clearer that way—less nervous rambling. Mama knew what had happened. But she was making Birdie do it.

Mama gave Birdie a pointed look. "Let's not leave anything out, okay?"

Birdie glanced to her armpit. The color navy showed sweat, something terrible. Keeping her integrity sure was a sweaty business. She took a deep breath. And then she began the story of how she'd come to find and almost keep a big pile of money that didn't belong to her.

After she finished, the officer asked Mr. Garrett if he wanted to press charges for Birdie's trespassing. Birdie nearly fell out of her chair, and even Mama looked taken aback.

"Absolutely, not," Mr. Garrett said.

After that the officer seemed to relax.

Mr. Garrett asked when the money could be returned to the victims, and the officer said he wasn't sure.

Birdie didn't know how she found the nerve, but she said, "My cousin thinks you're going to keep it. You're not going to keep it, are you?"

The officer leaned forward in his swivel chair. He looked deadly serious. "We don't do things like that here."

"Can I come with you? To return the money?" She had to be sure. "I'd like to say *sorry* to everyone."

The officer flexed a bicep and stuck out his lower lip, frowning.

"Let her come," said a tall, Black officer sitting nearby. "This kid needs to look those people in the eyes. See who she almost stole from."

The officer who had taken her statement shook his head. "You know there's a formal process, and we can't do that. Anyway, who would look after her to make sure she doesn't steal anything else?"

Now it was Birdie's turn to frown. "I'm not a thief. I'm here, aren't I?"

He stared at her a few seconds like he wasn't quite sure. Finally, he said, "I suppose you are."

Maybe white skin and a nice dress could only go so far. She'd been completely honest in her story. She'd told the officer she'd kept the money a little while— even after she'd read on the library's computer about it being stolen from the elderly. People judged you for what you'd done. Actions mattered. Maybe they mattered more than appearances.

Mama said doing the right thing was hard, and that it
wasn't easy for her either. "It would've been great to be
able to give my dad a nice funeral and afford new
clothes for a change. Believe me, I thought for a second
about keeping that freezer money. But I had to accept
that it wasn't ours. And as hard as it'll be, as soon as I
get a job, I'll have to pay back the $1,150 I spent even
though it'd be a lot easier if I didn't."

Birdie understood just how hard that would be for
Mama. She'd called Kellog to tell him she wouldn't
be sending him a box of money—that she'd given it to
the police. He'd wanted her to keep some. Such a pile of
money, no one would have noticed if a few hundreds

were missing. *You couldn't have sent me at least one bill?* he'd yelled.

"Maybe Kellog was right, and we shouldn't have given the money back—at least not all of it."

"Would you feel good about that?" Mama asked. "Keeping money from these families who've been scammed?"

"No." But she also didn't feel good about Kellog being mad at her.

Mama seemed to read her mind. "Kellog will get over this, just like we will."

If Kellog wanted money, a few days later Birdie had figured out a way to give him some. She went back to the library and traced a hundred-dollar bill she'd looked up on the computer screen onto a white piece of paper, but instead of Benjamin Franklin's face, she drew what she hoped looked like Kellog's face. And instead of *This Note Is Legal Tender for All Debts Public and Private*, which was written on the front of the real hundred, she wrote, This Note is Legal Tender for All Birdie's Debts and Wrongdoings. She colored it orange (Kellog's favorite color), cut it out, borrowed an envelope and stamp from Mama, and mailed it off. And the next day she mailed off another one, and every following day that she didn't hear from Kellog, she mailed another.

Word about the money had gotten around school. People asked Birdie what a half a million dollars looked like, how heavy it was, and if the criminals who'd escaped from jail were still looking for her.

Birdie didn't want to think about that final question.

Last period was history with Mr. Gladwell, and he went on and on about the Gilded Age, talking about the Vanderbilts' lavish display of wealth in a time when so many other people were so poor. It was hard not to make real-life comparisons. Jacob Powers was wearing this awesome black skater sweatshirt with white checkerboard on the sleeves, and Birdie couldn't help thinking how he could probably afford to buy Vans clothes like that anytime he wanted. And her mama had to scrub toilets just to afford thrift store clothes. And while she was done with lying and she didn't want to be a thief, she still couldn't quite get over how unfair it was that some people had so much and other people had so little.

But Jacob didn't seem to take her glaring at him personally, because when Mr. Gladwell's back was turned, a note folded into a tight triangle flew into the air and landed on her desk.

Birdie, I know you're still mad at me about the lake. But I'm not like Travis. Just because he's a jerk doesn't mean I am. He's always begging

to stay home and help my dad at the store
because he hates school. It makes him mean.
I'm not trying to make excuses for him. I'm just
telling you that family isn't always the same.
Please, let's hang out? I want to see what else
you can do on a board.

Birdie read the line about family again, because she couldn't stop thinking about her own family, and how if she'd decided to steal Mrs. Kirkland's ring or keep the money, she'd have ended up just like her father. But she didn't, so she wasn't.

And she and Mama had plans tomorrow to visit everyone the money belonged to so Birdie could say she was sorry. Mr. Garrett had agreed to share the list of names so Birdie could make amends. So even if she ended up poor for the rest of her life, at least she wasn't a thief. She was someone who did the right thing and apologized for her mistakes. She tore off a piece of paper from her notebook.

I get it. I'm not like everyone in my family either. We can hang out.

She folded it up and threw it into the air.

When she got home from school, there were a ton of people in Woodcroft's parking lot. Mama was standing in the crowd. She saw Birdie and ran to meet her.

"Jessie caught the thieves!" Mama shrieked.

"What? Really?!"

Mama hugged her close. "He sure did. On his way home from work he saw some guys coming out of the woods. He thought they looked suspicious, so he checked the escaped criminals' mugshots online, and sure enough, it was them. He had his gun and his handcuffs with him, so he had them sitting ready by the time the police arrived."

"Wow," Birdie said. Jessie had finally gotten his chance for excitement.

Jessie walked over. "Hey, Little Bird. People saw me on the news, so everyone wants to hear the story straight from the horse's mouth." After Jessie relayed what happened a few dozen times, he came back with Birdie and Mama to their apartment. Mama had made buckeyes and offered him some.

They sat around eating candy and talking about how mad it all was, Birdie's finding the money, and Jessie capturing the bad guys who'd stolen it. They were laughing with relief until Jessie got serious and told Birdie she'd done something really dangerous by not telling anybody the real story behind the money.

"You can't keep stuff like that to yourself, okay?" Jessie's eyes searched Birdie's, looking for her to reassure him.

Birdie nodded even though it seemed a one in a million chance something like this would ever happen again.

And if it was a different situation, right versus wrong might get jumbled up in her head again. "How do you always know the right thing to do?" She didn't think Jessie went to church.

Jessie shrugged. "It's not always easy. But I read a lot. I try to be kind, and I try to think through to the consequences of things."

Reading, *ugh*. "What kind of books? Thick, boring ones?" For some reason she imagined the old, leather-bound books in the Biltmore's library.

Jessie laughed. "No. If they're boring, I put them down. I like action. I read mysteries, true crime, sci-fi—only exciting books for me."

Birdie was surprised. "And you learn how to be a good person from books like that?"

"Sure. You learn how other people feel and get to experience their pain and hurt. See the world through enough people's eyes, and it'll change you."

"We better get going," Mama said. "We're meeting Mr. Garrett over in Evercrest."

Jessie nodded. "That seems like a real-life experience that'll change you."

38

As Mama and Birdie were gathering their things, the cat started meowing his head off. Birdie had just gotten home from school, and he didn't seem to like the idea of her leaving again so soon. So, Birdie picked him up. "Can we take him?" Birdie hugged the cat close. She needed him. Mr. Garrett had spent the week tracking down the current addresses of the people affected by his nephews' investment scam, and now they were going to make amends.

They met Mr. Garrett at the first house on his list. It was owned by a woman named Eula Wellesley. She lived on the same street as Mrs. Hillmore, and Birdie cringed to be so close to the place where she had caused Mama to lose her job.

Like Mrs. Hillmore's and all the houses in Evercrest, Ms. Wellesley's house was of the oversized variety. Ms. Wellesley sure didn't seem like she was hurting for money. Birdie felt a small stab of regret. All that money would be going back to people who didn't need it instead of to people like her and Mama or Aunt Laura and Kellog.

Birdie forced herself out of the car with the cat snuggled into her neck.

Mr. Garrett rang the bell. Though they could hear movement inside, it seemed like forever before someone opened the door. Finally, Ms. Wellesley emerged, hunched heavily over a walker. "You better not be trying to sell me something," she said before anyone spoke. "I can't eat candy, and I don't like magazines."

"Sorry to bother you, ma'am," Mr. Garrett explained. "We're here to talk to you about the money you lost in the lake house scam my nephews invented. Do you remember me from the courthouse?"

Ms. Wellesley squinted at him like she wasn't sure. She had the door propped open only as wide as her walker, and she seemed not terribly inclined to open it further until she laid eyes on Birdie's cat.

Mr. Garrett motioned to Birdie. "This young lady found part of your money that was taken."

"Awww, what a sweet-looking cat." She leaned in, widening the door. "What's his name?"

"Jackpot," Birdie said without thinking about it first. "He helped me find the money."

Ms. Wellesley nodded like this made perfect sense. "Why don't you all come inside since instead of taking my money, you seem to want to give me some."

They stepped in, and Birdie told the whole crazy story again, all the while rubbing the cat's soft fur to help her get through it. She admitted her part in finding the money and almost keeping it for her and Mama. She was too nervous to look Ms. Wellesley in the eye like Mama had said she should, but she did say, "I'm sorry," like she had promised.

After that Ms. Wellesley offered Jackpot a bowl of water and a bite of tuna. She said she used to have a cat, and she missed her a lot. "Animals won't do you wrong like people will. I haven't gotten another one because my health isn't too good these days. I can't commit to another animal right now."

They all sat down, and Ms. Wellesley told her story of how Mr. Garrett's nephews had convinced her that she could double her retirement money investing in lake houses in Florida. "The real estate market is so much better in Florida than it is here. And those young men lived right down the road. I wouldn't have thought anyone living in Evercrest wasn't trustworthy. I learned my lesson, though. I don't trust anybody now."

Ms. Wellesley said they'd stolen $350,000 from her.

"I'm so sorry," Mr. Garrett said. "I hope the police will be able to give you back at least some of it."

At first Ms. Wellesley seemed upset about only getting back what she called a *small amount*—if the police divided the money equally among the victims. It still seemed like a lot to Birdie, but she understood how if something belonged to you, you'd want it back. She'd felt it when she thought Mrs. Kirkland had taken her money (that wasn't her money) from the treehouse.

Jackpot finished his tuna and wandered around, hopping into Ms. Wellesley's lap. Ms. Wellesley stroked the cat's back. "I haven't told that story since the courtroom. I told my son when it first happened, but of course, he yelled at me for being so stupid." She shook her head.

"You weren't stupid," Birdie insisted. "You trusted that the world was a good place, and there's nothing wrong with that."

Ms. Wellesley stroked the cat's back. "I guess."

It bothered her that Ms. Wellesley didn't trust anyone. "I wasn't trustworthy—I know that, and the criminals weren't trustworthy, but I think most people are. Like my mama"—Birdie motioned to Mama who sat quietly beside her, because it was Birdie's story to tell— "and me from now on. I'm not going to be a liar anymore." She looked Ms. Wellesley in the eye when she said that. "I promise."

Ms. Wellesley smiled for the first time since they'd gotten there.

Birdie nodded at Jackpot. "He's a good cat, isn't he?"

"He is."

And for the first time since they got there, Birdie smiled, too.

Birdie, Mr. Garrett, and Mama went door to door until dark, greeting the skeptical victims of the lake house investment scam. Some people were nice. Some people were grouchy. Some people were mad. Some were surprised—a lot were surprised. Seemed like most people didn't think they'd ever see a cent of the money they'd lost. But one man seemed to expect every last one. He yelled into Mr. Garrett's face that he better get out there right now and find the rest of his money *or else.* And if Birdie wasn't scared straight before, she was after that.

Mama put her arm around Birdie's shoulders and squeezed. "I'm proud of you. Even if people don't appreciate it, you're doing the right thing."

Birdie sure hoped so.

Because she told her story over and over, saying she was sorry and admitting each time her deception. Mama was there after every house to hug her again and tell her she was doing good. She didn't need Mama to say it, though. Because it stopped mattering how people responded. What began to matter more was how telling her story made her feel. With each telling, the good, honest person she wanted to be became more true. With each *I'm sorry*, her integrity returned to her bit by bit, filling her up with a kind of goodness like she felt when she snuggled her cat. On the last house, though, she handed Jackpot to Mama and asked her to wait in the car.

"You don't want to take him in?" she asked.

"I got this on my own now. I know you guys will be here when I get back."

And they were. That was something she could trust.

But when the last house on Mr. Garrett's list had been checked off, and they returned to Woodcroft, a rent-due notice hung from their front door. "I thought we paid the rent," Birdie said.

"We did," Mama said. "Unfortunately, it's a new month."

"The rent is due again already?" Birdie asked.

"Looks like it." Mama took the notice off the door and pushed it deep in her purse. Doing the right thing hadn't come with a reward, and there was no more money hidden in the freezer.

39

Birdie couldn't stop thinking about two things: the people she'd given the money to, and the fact that she and Mama still needed money. Finally, they collided in Birdie's mind, and she borrowed Mama's phone to call Mr. Garrett. She asked if he would share the list of names and addresses of all the people they'd met, and she told him her plan to get money for her and Mama.

He agreed and was nice enough to lend her some postage stamps, because she needed them. She promised to pay him back, but he insisted she could have them for free.

Then Birdie borrowed some of Mama's fancy stationery and started writing.

Dear Ms. Wellesley,

This is Birdie, the girl who found your stolen money hidden in a wall. You met me the other day. I'm writing to tell you about my mama, Janey Loggerman, who was there with me, too. She is amazing at cleaning. She leaves no crumb behind and no surface unscrubbed. She can fold clothes better than the Gap and organize your pantry like a grocery store shelf. She's kind and trustworthy. If you'd like to hire her, I'm including her phone number below.

Sincerely,

Birdie Loggerman

Birdie put her words in an envelope with the correct address and a stamp, and then she wrote the same letter to the next name on the list. Again and again until she had written fifty letters. Then she spent a good ten minutes outside putting each one through the thin outgoing mail slot.

Two days later Birdie sunk her teeth into a juicy cheeseburger that Jessie had cooked on his small charcoal grill. He'd set it up in the tall-weeded area by the trampoline and placed three folding chairs around it for them to sit. Birdie couldn't remember the last time she'd had a burger this good. Probably never. Yes, it was the best burger of her life. "This is amazing," Birdie said.

Mama looked like she was about to agree when her phone interrupted them. "Do you guys mind if I take this?"

"Nah, go ahead," Jessie said. He scooped another burger from the grill onto a bun.

"Yes, this is Janey . . . Yes, I can come tomorrow. Hang on. Let me get a pen so I can write that down." Mama ran inside their apartment.

When she returned there was a huge smile on her face.

"Who was that?" Birdie asked.

"Verna Keats. She wants me to clean her house tomorrow. She says you sent her a letter?"

Birdie grinned, but before she could say anything Mama's phone rang again.

"Sorry, I guess I better take this." Mama disappeared back into the apartment.

Jessie set down his burger. "What's that all about, Little Bird?"

Birdie broke off a tiny piece of meat for Jackpot. The cat gobbled it off her fingers, then rubbed himself appreciatively along her legs. "Oh, I just sent out some letters telling all the people I met the other day that Mama is a great cleaner."

"Wow." Jessie looked impressed. "Clever girl."

After a few minutes Mama came back outside. "Well, imagine that. My phone rang and rang, then rang again. I am booked solid for next week!"

"Woo-hoo!" Birdie jumped in the air.

"And Eula Wellesley wants you to come with me and bring the cat."

"Really? She wants me to bring Jackpot?"

Mama nodded. "Would you be willing to do that?"

"Jackpot will love it." And she would, too. Since she'd gotten in trouble at Mrs. Hillmore's house, she hadn't thought she'd be allowed at any of Mama's jobs anymore. She was glad to be invited along.

Mama's phone continued to ring until Birdie's bedtime. And the next morning before she went to school, it rang twice more. And when Birdie got home from school, Mama said before Birdie could even set down her book-bag, "We have a problem."

"A problem?" Birdie stood at the door, wondering if the electric bill was overdue or if the car had broken down.

"My phone hasn't stopped ringing with people wanting me to clean."

"That's not a problem. That's great!"

"Yes, but I can't do all these jobs. I'm having to turn people down."

"Don't do that!" Birdie shouted.

"Okay. Come on inside and put your bag down. We'll figure this out."

At the kitchen table, Birdie and Mama discussed what to do about the fact that Mama had gone from having no job to having too many jobs.

"What about Aunt Laura? Could she clean some of the houses?" Birdie asked.

"I don't know. She has her job at the restaurant. I'm not sure if she'd want to quit and move up here. But maybe." Mama looked thoughtful. "But even with Aunt Laura's help, I'd have to turn down a lot of people."

"Do you know anyone else who needs a job?"

"Lavonne who lives downstairs has been looking for work for months. I don't know if she knows how to clean houses, though."

"You can teach her. Bring her with you to your jobs next week and show her what to do." Birdie slapped the table. "What if you start your own company like Clean as a Whistle? You can have a team of cleaners working for you."

Mama beamed at Birdie. "You're jam-packed full of good ideas today. And Aunt Laura would be a lot more interested in helping if I told her we were starting a company together. She's better with numbers than I am. She could help me with the accounting, and I could manage the employees."

The next day was Saturday, and Hailey made a surprise visit.

She stood on the concrete landing outside Birdie's front door in a purple-and-yellow leotard with rhinestones. "I thought we could hang out."

"Did gymnastics get cancelled?" Birdie craned around Hailey to see if Mrs. Kirkland was there, too, but she didn't see her. It seemed strange that Hailey's mom would drop her off at Woodcroft after the fuss she'd made over it.

"No. I'm skipping. I used the Ryde app to get here."

"Wow. Your mom let you do that?"

"No. She doesn't know."

"Oh." Birdie got a bad feeling like she did when she lied—like she was about to make a mess of things. Only this wasn't her lie, so did that mean it wasn't her mess? Hailey's messes often ended up being her messes. "What if your mom finds out you're here and blames me?"

"She's not going to find out."

"Well, she found out about the lake, and then, she told you couldn't be friends with me anymore."

"Are you saying I should go home?"

"Who's going home?" Mama asked. She and Jessie had joined them at the door.

Birdie gave Hailey a long look. "It's not that I don't want you to come over, because I do."

"Did you girls have a disagreement?"

Hailey shook her head. "No, Ms. Loggerman. Everything's okay with us. But can I ask you to take me home?"

Mama looked from Birdie to Hailey, back to Birdie. "Well, didn't you just get here? Birdie, are you not inviting your friend inside?"

"No, I'm not." Birdie gave Hailey a hard look. She loved her friend, but she couldn't stand the idea of being in trouble again.

"It's my fault, Ms. Loggerman. My mom doesn't know I'm here."

"Oh." Mama's face lit with understanding. "Okay, come on. I'll take you home."

In the car on the way to Hailey's house, Birdie glanced at her friend to see if she might be mad, but Hailey grabbed her hand and squeezed it. "Sorry. You're right. I shouldn't have come."

"Oh man, you really shouldn't have."

Because when they pulled into Hailey's driveway, Mrs. Kirkland stood outside of her car like she'd just gotten home. "Hailey?"

Hailey jumped out. "Mom, I thought you had Pilates. What are you doing here?"

"Your dad needs me to scan a document he forgot to bring on his trip. What are *you* doing is the better question. Why aren't you at gymnastics?"

"I skipped. But Birdie had nothing to do with it, and I asked Ms. Loggerman to bring me home when I realized it was the wrong thing to do."

Mrs. Kirkland walked over to Mama's side of the car.

Mama rolled down the window.

Mrs. Kirkland leaned in, her eyes soft. "Thank you for bringing her home." The fury quickly returned to her face. "Hailey, in the house. Now."

Hailey waved and ran inside.

Mama turned to Birdie. "Looks like Hailey is in real trouble."

"Yeah," Birdie agreed. "I feel bad for her. It might be the first time she's ever been in real trouble. I guess even rich kids get it wrong sometimes."

Money didn't seem to make knowing right from wrong any easier.

Birdie was at Ms. Wellesley's house reading her a book while Jackpot sat on Ms. Wellesley's lap getting his fur rubbed. Ms. Wellesley said her neck bothered her to read, so she had Birdie get a book from the bookshelf to read aloud. But the only books Ms. Wellesley had were romances, and Birdie couldn't help making faces at the kissing parts, and when she got to the more-than-kissing parts, her face lit up with heat, and she stumbled over the words.

"Okay, that's enough," Ms. Wellesley said, adjusting herself on the sofa. "I have an idea. Why don't you pick out a book you want to read? My nephew in Washington loves a book called *The Lightning Thief*. I bought him the whole series. You could get that one, or whatever you want."

"I might grab a different one." She'd had enough of thieving in real life. She didn't need to read about it even if all her friends were.

"Maybe you can stop at the library before you come next time and pick something up."

"You want me to come again next time?"

"If you don't mind. I enjoy your company. And Jackpot's. And I'll pay you to read to me."

"Pay me?"

"How's ten dollars an hour?"

"Are you serious?" Birdie asked, incredulous.

"Okay, eleven dollars. You're eleven years old, so I think eleven dollars is fair. And that'll include your trip to the library. I'm not paying extra for that."

"Yes, ma'am." Birdie nodded. It was all she could do to keep her cool. She'd never made her own money. Eleven whole dollars an hour. It was a fortune. Well, okay, it wasn't half a million dollars hidden-in-a-wall fortune, but still, it was a lot—enough to make her smile the whole ride home.

40

A month later Birdie was at a pet shelter helping Kellog pick out a dog. "Oh my gosh, look at this sweet face," Birdie gushed. The dog had black-marble eyes, a carrot-shaped nose, and caramel-colored fur.

Patrick, the guy helping them, opened carrot-nose's cage to let them interact with the dog. Aunt Laura stood back checking her phone, which was blowing up with messages for the cleaning business. Mama and Aunt Laura had a tendency to do more than clean people's houses. They kind of managed their lives.

"Hey, little guy," Kellog said. They both sat down on the floor to see if the dog would come to them.

Carrot-nose raced over and excitedly began licking Kellog's hand. "He'd make a great lap dog."

"He would," Birdie agreed. That was what they needed. Mama and Aunt Laura had several clients who'd requested a dog to pet while they got their house cleaned. Word had gotten out about Birdie bringing Jackpot to sit with Ms. Wellesley, and pet therapy had become an unofficial perk of having your house cleaned by Loggerwomen Cleaners. Jackpot had made the rounds, getting love from lots of folks. But demand was high, and Birdie and Jackpot could only be in one place at a time. So, Aunt Laura had agreed to let Kellog get a dog if he would bring him over to her clients' houses after school to sit on laps and get petted.

A dog was going to be good for Kellog. He and Aunt Laura lived in Woodcroft in an apartment two rows over from her and Mama, and she and Kellog got to skateboard together every weekend. Jacob and Samiya had even started joining them.

They'd found Samiya's ring in the bowling alley at the Biltmore House, and she'd apologized that everyone thought Birdie had taken it. Birdie had an easy time forgiving her and invited Samiya to learn to skateboard. Kellog was still struggling with having to leave all his other friends behind in Polkville, so it was good for him to meet more of Birdie's friends. It hadn't been that long ago that Birdie had been the new kid. She understood that it took some getting used to.

Birdie turned to her cousin. "What do you think? He seems the friendliest."

Carrot-nose hadn't stopped licking Kellog's hand.

Kellog nodded. "He's the one."

Aunt Laura looked up from her phone and turned to Patrick. "We'll take him."

When Birdie got home, she curled up in her bed with Jackpot and cracked open a book. An actual book not assigned to her by a teacher. She'd gone to the library to find something to read to Ms. Wellesley, and that smiley librarian with the snake tattoo had noticed her skateboard. She'd told Birdie that she had a great book about Roller Derby. Roller-skating and skateboarding weren't exactly the same thing, so Birdie had been skeptical. But the book had pictures. So instead of *The Lightning Thief*, Birdie had left the library with *Roller Girl*. She'd been reading it to Ms. Wellesley and bringing it home to read ahead because she couldn't wait to see what happened, which meant she still hadn't actually read *The Lightning Thief*.

So, when the girls were discussing which Greek god would be the best to have for a parent, Birdie had braved mentioning that she hadn't read that book. There was a lot of shouting and carrying on from Lily and Samiya who said they couldn't believe it. How in the world had Birdie not read *The Lightning Thief*?

But Birdie just said, "Believe it," and took *Roller Girl* from her bookbag. "I'm reading this," she said. "It's about this girl who suddenly starts competing at roller-skating even though she's not very good at it."

And that changed the subject to talking about Samiya and her newfound obsession with skateboarding, which led Hailey to accuse Samiya of only taking up skateboarding because she thought Kellog was cute.

Samiya didn't deny it, which was gross, but whatever. Birdie was just happy to have friends to skateboard with again.

A few weeks later Lily invited the girls on a service project, organizing stuff for a huge yard sale to benefit Habitat for Humanity. It was on a Saturday, which was the same day as gymnastics, but Lily said she had no problem missing a day of gymnastics to do a good deed. Samiya said she didn't mind either. But Hailey said there was no way her mom was going to let her miss gymnastics, and that Birdie wouldn't let her skip. She gave Birdie a sly smile when she said this, like she was teasing her. "Whenever I do something bad, Birdie gets in trouble."

"It's true!" Birdie shrieked. And everyone had laughed.

So, it ended up only three of them with masking tape and markers, making up prices for old toys and clothes, helping someone else own a home.

Birdie wore her trusty skateboarding pants with the sewn-shut pockets. Of course, Mama had bought her newer pants, but these seemed the best for shuffling against dusty items from people's attics. Forgetting she didn't have pockets, she tried to stuff the marker in them. She needed a place to put it while she opened another box of junk that needed organizing and pricing. Of course, she was greeted with only one small pocket that still contained the silver button from Lily's dress. She took it out of its tiny hiding place without thinking about it, and Samiya noticed.

"What's that?" Samiya asked.

"It's a button from the navy dress Lily gave me."

"Really?" Lily leaned in to look. The button was no longer very sparkly or very silvery. It really didn't look like the same button. Lily looked skeptical. "Did it fall off?"

"No, I cut it off," Birdie admitted. "The dress didn't fit, but I really loved it, so I cut off a button."

"It didn't fit?" Lily looked shocked.

"None of the clothes you gave me fit. And I felt sad or mad . . . or both, so I decided to carry around a silver button to remind myself how miserable I was about it."

"Well, that sounds awful," Samiya said.

Birdie nodded. "It does, doesn't it?"

"You should throw it away," Lily said.

"Maybe." They worked in silence for a few minutes. Finally, Birdie decided something. "The whole thing was embarrassing, but I like that it reminds me of who I want to be. I don't want to forget." She rolled the button between her fingers. "I'm going to keep it." Maybe someday she'd throw it away, but for now, she wanted to remember she wasn't a girl who stole things.

"How would you forget who you want to be?" Lily asked.

"I don't know. I get caught up in keeping up with you guys." She eyed the girls to see how they would react to this.

"I understand what she means. It's hard when you're different. You want to hide it. Like I'm a Hindu, but I didn't used to talk about it. Then I wondered if that made me not really me. So, when we did that cultural diversity unit, I decided to speak up."

"You did a really good job," Birdie said.

Lily hadn't been there, and for a second, she looked a little horrified. Like she hadn't realized the whole world didn't have the same religion she did. But she recovered quickly. "I guess it's like how I listen to heavy metal. Well, I like this one Japanese band called Babymetal—not like *all* heavy metal. Anyway, I feel bad about it, like I should be listening to Christian music instead, but I really like it, so I can't seem to stop."

"Why should you stop? Are you afraid God is going to judge you?" Samiya asked.

"I guess," Lily said.

"Well, I can't speak for the heavens, but I won't judge you," Birdie said.

"Me either," Samiya agreed.

Lily laughed. "Friendship pact: no judging allowed." She stuck out her pinky finger, and Birdie latched on.

"No lying or withholding important things either?" Birdie asked.

"Deal," said the girls.

"We'll rope Hailey into this agreement on Monday. We won't see her tomorrow either, because she's training for a meet," Lily said.

"Oh, she's in," Birdie said. "I'll make sure of it."

Later that evening Birdie thought about the *no withholding information* part of the pact, and after watching their *Let's Go Home* episode, she brought it up with Mama. "You know how I said I won't lie anymore?"

Mama gave her the side eye like she wasn't sure she liked where this conversation was going. "Yeah."

"But you always said I could lie about Rick if I had to?"

Mama turned all the way around to face her on the couch. Birdie had her full attention. "Yes."

"Well, what if I don't want to? What if I want to talk about him?"

"Talk about him how? What would you say?"

"Like how he's in prison and that stinks. And I wish he wasn't. Or that I wish I had a good dad like Hailey's or Lily's."

"Oh. Well, Rick wasn't all bad. He did sweet things sometimes. He gave the best foot rubs when I was pregnant with you."

"He did?"

"Uh-huh. And he cooked for me when my feet hurt, too. But he's in prison now, and I want you to think about how Mrs. Kirkland judged you for where you live. What are your friends going to say if you tell them your father's in jail?"

"I don't know. But I think if they're my friends, they'll say something nice."

Mama nodded. "They should. But people aren't always as nice as we'd hope."

"Well, if they aren't nice, I don't want them as friends."

Mama looked impressed. "Okay. But what are you going to do if Mrs. Kirkland finds out?"

"After all that drama at her house, do you really think there's anything else that could shock her?"

Mama laughed. "No. But that doesn't mean she won't say you and Hailey can't be friends."

"I know. But if Hailey's really my friend, we'll find a way."

Mama nodded okay. "If you're willing to risk it, you have my blessing."

"The truth is important to me," Birdie said. "I pinky-swore on it."

"A pinky swear? My goodness, why didn't you say so?" Mama stuck out her pinky finger.

There was a warm patch of sun on the couch near Mama. Birdie slid into it and grabbed Mama's pinky with hers.

Mama smiled.

Birdie smiled, too.

And when Mama wouldn't give Birdie's finger back, they sank into the couch laughing.

RECIPE FOR BIRDIE'S BUCKEYES

Makes 5 dozen

INGREDIENTS
½ cup peanut butter

1 cup butter, softened

½ teaspoon vanilla extract

6 cups confectioners' sugar

4 cups semisweet chocolate chips

In a large bowl, blend together peanut butter, butter, vanilla extract, and sugar. Roll dry dough into 1-inch balls and place on a cookie sheet lined with parchment paper.

Place a toothpick into each ball for dipping later. Put the cookie sheet in the freezer for 30 minutes (don't forget!).

In a double broiler, melt the chocolate chips on medium-low heat for approximately 5 minutes, stirring until smooth.

Holding on to the toothpick, dip each frozen peanut butter ball in chocolate. Leave a small round portion of peanut butter showing at the top to make the treats look like eyes. Put them back on the cookie sheet and refrigerate until serving.

ACKNOWLEDGMENTS

My endless gratitude to my Tuesday night gals: Victoria Beck, Georgia Bragg, Christine Bernardi, Tracy Holczer, Leslie Margolis, Elizabeth Passerelli, Anne Reinhard, and Laurie Young, who listened, encouraged, and gave feedback on every page of this book. For the pudding sisters, Rita Huang Crayon, Frances Sackett, and Lori Snyder, who also read, encouraged, and gave notes that made the book so much better than it ever would have been if it were just me.

So much love to the ladybugs: Bridget Casey, Hannah Hudson, and Kristi Olson, who never hesitate to read for me when I ask. Huge thanks to Melanie Crowder, whose course on emotion through the Writing Barn put many new tricks up my writing sleeve. Gratitude to Jules Jones, who talked plot with me and Elana Arnold, who walked with me. Thanks to Anindita Basu Sempere and Kimberley Gorelik Moran, who read the bits and pieces I needed them to.

A thousand thanks to Stephanie Fretwell-Hill, who believed in me and Birdie and is always there to answer my questions. Enormous gratitude to Susan Dobinick for such thoughtful notes and for being such a huge champion of my work. Thank you to Allison Moore for also loving Birdie's story and being willing to take me under her wing. To Shannon Harts and Diane Aronson for such thorough copyedits. To the amazing team at Bloomsbury that helps get the word out: Ksenia Winnicki, Phoebe Dyer, Beth Eller, and Jasmine Miranda. Also, thanks to designer Jeanette Levy and creative director Donna Mark for your help with the book. And to Julia Bereciartu for the most amazing cover art I could have dreamed up.

Thank you to Janifer Joel, who told me a crazy, true story that inspired the idea for this book. Gratitude to my parents. I'm in awe of how you managed to raise my sister and me under such difficult circumstances.

To my husband, whom I count on for last-minute reads and who's gotten so darn good at giving feedback. I love you always, and I will forever be inspired by you.